For
Mary Schultz
Be sure to share
a favour the wolf track
all the way
along

[signature]
TCBF. St Fr.
Oct 14, 2017

LAKE STORIES
& other tales

BY TIM JOLLYMORE
AVAILABLE FROM FINNS WAY BOOKS

Listener in the Snow

Observation Hill, a novel of class and murder

The Advent of Elizabeth

Lake Stories and Other Tales

12: Booze (2017)

In memory of
Klaus Jankofsky,
my professor

LAKE STORIES
& other tales

TIM JOLLYMORE

FINNS WAY
B O O K S

Printed in the United States of America. For information, address Finns Way Books™, 360 Grand Avenue, Suite 204, Oakland, California, 94610; or contact www.finnswaybooks.com

For information on Finns Way Reading Group Guides, please contact Finns Way Books™ by electronic mail at readinggroupguides@finnswaybooks.com

ISBN 978-0-9914763-7-4

January 17, 2016

Contents

§

WOLVES DANCE

§

GOING DOWNTOWN

§

TIMBER

§

NEXT ROOM

§

FEDERAL CASE

WOLF'S END

§

LAKE STORIES
& other tales

Wolves Dance

Wolves dance
with the stars.
They do the Borealis,
a six-step
cold-rumba
up on hinders,
pawing a nor'easter,
spinning, tails up,
to the beat
of Orion's still frozen drum.
Starlit eyes
wallow in their heads.

Nature Boy

1 *Nature Boy*

THE RICE LAKE ROAD LEAVES TOWN, passes through jack pine woods checkered by a few farm fields, through the Fond du Lac Reservation, curves in what was at one time a vicious S three miles past the tribal headquarters, then rolls straight to the northern shore of the lake where the casino-rich *Anishinabe* bought and have returned to open space Chet Pelton's Resort. Pelton's had been a place where the boy's family spent two weeks each year between the hottest part of July and the aquatic-blooming dog days of August.

During one of those early summers, the boy, now six, and his mother were making the trip to town in the tomato-soup-and-cracker car, a 1955 two-toned Pontiac. It was out of the crumpled body of that white-top car that his father, while his luck held out, would walk away without a scratch. The boy would remember the car not by his shock at seeing its smashed wreck—his father's handiwork—on a trailer in the garage of Bolten's Salvage but by the feel of fresh air that passed so sweetly through the wing windows of the car this July morning. The two-year-old Pontiac was heavy and cruised the road smoothly under his mother's steady hands.

The boy slid next to her on the bench seat to watch her drive. As she handled the wheel, the fine hairs of her slender forearms shifted in the early breezes, her curls

3

brushed her neck and pushed away from her tanned face. She mostly regarded the road but twice turned to smile down at him. She reached out one hand, tousling his hair that had finally grown out from the June summer-cut his father insisted all the boys get. He watched the fine hairs on her arm shift and dance with the wind. A golden sun filtered through the pines, lighting those hairs as they waved one way, then, ensemble again in another direction like the schools of lake minnows he had watched from the dock. Now light, now dark. Now one way, now the next. The delicate movements mesmerized him.

An unusual-looking man off to one side of the road caught the boy's eye. "Who is that?" He pointed.

Stripped to the waist, solidly tan, his blond hair flowing golden over his dark, bulky shoulder blades, he sat erect in the tractor seat. His extended arms twined rapidly, hand over hand, steering around the end of a furrow. He was harrowing weeds from potato vines in one of the infrequent pine-bound fields. Straight backed, the half-naked figure, leaving one hand on the tractor steerage, twisted his trim torso to reach back with the other hand, lifting a leg above and straddling the high seat, sidesaddle, to look down both at where he was going and to where he had harrowed. His chest bulged between his outstretched arms. He did not look up as they passed. The boy followed the man's work, first craning his neck, then getting up on his knees to look out the Pontiac's rear window, gathering in the sight. "Who is that?"

Without as much as a glance away from the road ahead she answered him. "Oh, that's Nature Boy."

"Who?"

"Just a man who tends the Linnemakis' fields and garden." She continued to look at the road ahead. "Have you thought about what treat I'll get you at the store?"

He hadn't, but now the image of a cylinder of frozen cream, orange and white, cooling and sweet, pushed the tractor man from his mind.

"I would like a push-up, I think."

He returned her smile. He didn't think of Nature Boy until he saw him again.

Their trips back and forth to town were not frequent, but happened often enough that year and the next for the boy to form a ritual, to establish a tradition of looking for Nature Boy.

"There's Nature Boy," he would announce.

When the man was not to be seen, the boy said nothing. He did feel a little glum when he missed sighting the familiar character. Where was he when not working the garden? The thought fascinated him. Nature Boy never looked at them as the car passed. He always paid attention to his work and was always atop the tractor, turned slightly in the seat looking back at what his equipment was doing. Every time, he rode bare to the waist. Even early in the year, his muscular shoulders and chest were tanned. In hot weather the man wore shorts of a tied-on, toga-like variety, something the boy had never seen other men wear in those days.

"There's Nature Boy."

The first time the following summer, the man was turning the soil. The boy began his questions.

"Does he live in that house?"

"No, the Linnemakis live there."

"Where does he live?"

"I don't really know."

"Doesn't he have a home?"

His mother pushed the boy's shoulder lightly. "You *are* a curious one. Well, they say he built a cabin somewhere out in the woods there."

His pestering did not seem to bother her, but, when he persisted, she reddened, simply smiled, and kept her eyes fixed on the road. His ritual seemed to please her.

"Does he have a bathroom?"

"I suppose so."

She guided the Pontiac carefully round the tight curve leaving Nature Boy behind, tending his work.

"It's best to go slow right here," she told him. "These curves have killed people."

"Who?" He had forgotten Nature Boy again.

"I don't know the names, but it could happen again."

True. The S-curve was treacherous. From town, the road ran five straight miles, jogged suddenly more than fifty feet right, then jogged back again before it ran straight once more. Pines and muskeg bogs pressed the ditches close to the narrow shoulders. Some said Mick Curtis's Tavern, set an eighth mile past the curve, was to blame for the accidents. Mick, being surrounded by reservation land, habitually closed later than the town bars. More than once on a hot summer night, a spectacular crash erupted there in the wee hours, just before closing time: someone doing, they said, 100 miles an hour, blind drunk; or souped-up roadsters racing to the lake; or someone trying to make the last call at Mick's flying straight off the road. A hurtling Chevy or Ford left the road at the curve, rolled and tumbled over deep ditches, battered down pines, and strewed the muskeg swamps with bodies and muffled groans. One day, his father would be found there.

When the boy was nine, his family suspended their cabin stays at Chet Pelton's. They ceased passing back and forth on the road. Several years went by without him seeing Nature Boy. But later there were other reasons to go to the lake, although less frequently. Uncle Roy and Aunt Lavinia bought a white clapboard-sided, knotty pine lined cabin there, staying, at first in summer, then, permanently in a year-round house built with floor heat and a spacious kitchen. His father drove on those visits to his sister's cabin. Only once on any of these trips, the boy—now long past being a child—thrilled at his sighting. "There's Nature Boy!"

A silence as cold as a January drive with windows down flowed from the front seat and froze him in place. His mother stared straight ahead. His father rolled up his window, putting glass between him and Nature Boy. The boy's sudden fear in the cold of that moment told him not to pester. As he watched Nature Boy following the furrows, the man, not glancing at the road, shook his blonde mane across his shoulders, and continued steadily guiding the tractor.

The next summer, Jalmar Swenson built the go-cart track out near the lake. That brought the boy with his older brothers and friends past the Linnemaki farm. A five-minute go-cart ride cost a dollar—fifty cents if you were twelve or under—so the trips were many. He looked for Nature Boy each time he passed. The boy wondered which of his companions knew the half-naked, bronzed man, but he did not ask.

Instead, he invented legends about Nature Boy: Nature Boy never spoke. He lived alone in a shack made of bark and moss. He found injured animals and nursed them back to health. Mosquitoes did not bite him. He had appeared suddenly, out of nowhere, at the Linnemaki farm. He hiked down from Canada. The boy kept such stories to himself.

A few years later, the boy and a group of high school friends frequented another resort on the same lake. Kormie's was the summer spot. The girls one class above him driving by in their father's cars often stopped for him along the road to the lake. The cars were full of giggling, poking, and teasing. He crowded in and bashfully watched the girls. Among them he had his favorites, but he kept true in heart to a secret sweetheart from his own class. She never traveled in those cars.

These vacation friends all picnicked and tanned on the beach together, browning deeply in the first weeks of summer. He swam with the girls. They held a luau, playing as if they were exotic Hawaiians rather than small town Midwesterners.

He barely noticed Nature Boy working his field. The man did not look at the cars full of laughing girls that passed by. The girls teased the boy. "Oh, you look just like Nature Boy, so tan and strong." Over the sound of the tractor, Nature Boy seemed not to hear the merriment and shouts.

His junior year, the boy took up with La Rue, a rock and roll drummer and wild country kid, who lived out on Rice Lake Road. Even though the La Rue family's property bordered the Linnemakis' back forty, not once that year was the name of Nature Boy, who lived so close, uttered. The boy could have easily cleared up all mystery, but he had forgotten. His life was different. The road to his friend's house swept him away from what now would seem idle imagining.

That year surveyors and road graders came to wrest some of the danger from the tight S curve in the Rice Lake Road. Workers calmed its severe lines, tamed its menacing forces by banking the turns, and widened the shoulder as much as possible. The work lasted all the summer, but by autumn, the graders at the curve left behind them plenty of treachery for the unwary driver.

It was that same year his mother fought her first bout with cancer. Fear fell heavily on the boy. He watched her every move, examined each word for news. During her treatment, his father spun far off into his own darkness.

First came the terrifying news. Then the brutal removal: breast, skin, lymph nodes, muscle. He knew little of it, but his imagination filled his fears. Waiting for her return, his father cast gloom and worry about the house. No one spoke.

Then she stood before the boy at the kitchen doorway: a wreck, thin and blasted, inching her arm upward along the jamb, grunting, breathing heavily, and moaning the pain out. She reached up her forearm—she eventually worked it flat to the wood—scourged by the radiation, red, splotchy, raw. No fine hair shifted or grew there now.

He watched her chart the pain-filled efforts, week by week, bit by bit, up the kitchen doorjamb. She was to stretch and build atrophied muscles. At first, in agony, her hand barely made hip, then rib height. Later, she advanced her reach, giving out great groans, to as high as her shoulder, then above her head, in hope to heaven. Her grimacing subsided, and her breathing smoothed. She lengthened further. Finally, when her fully-extended arm, thin but now returned to its natural hue, lay up along the board and she could nearly touch the lintel overhead, she took her chart down. She folded it carefully and placed it in the drawer of her sewing machine cabinet.

Before he moved to his dorm room, she had started driving again. On his weekend visits from college, she took him up the lake road to a golf course Jalmar had built over the old go-cart track that, though mostly taken up or covered by turf, could still be seen past the 9th hole. There was the section of hairpin turn, which had incited his brothers' acceleration, baldly showing through the grasses that grew tightly around and little by little into the asphalt.

Golf was therapy for them both. She was returning to health; he was restoring his faith in her. He watched her careful swing. She did not wince, though after a nine-hole round, she was spent. He drove the ten miles back.

"There's Nature Boy," he said.

She spoke softly, almost to herself. He strained to decipher her whispers, then tried to draw her fully into conversation. "I used to make up stories, concoct theories about him. Who he was, where he came from."

Silent, she looked out at Linnemakis' field.

Her silence pricked him. "Still at it, isn't he?" He laughed. He gave the sighting a matter-of-fact sound.

"Yes," she said to the window, "he's still at it."

She watched as they passed. He drove. Then she relaxed against the seat, her eyes closed. She slept the rest of the way home. He kept his eye on her; she breathed easily, peacefully. The outing had put color in her cheeks; she looked lovely and content.

The second cancer came four years later. It seemed, from his distance at least, less brutal, less scary, but still difficult, especially alone. Perhaps if his father had careened off the Rice Lake Road after the surveyors and graders returned once again instead of going off the narrower treachery they left behind the first time, she would not have been alone. His father had not walked free the second time. He missed her second surgery. Only the determination to live kept her company.

It was after his father buried a Buick in the swamp west of the S curve that the county funded its monumental project. They filled and widened the Rice Lake Road. Out toward the lake, Nature Boy might have felt crowded and harried. The earlier work had stopped at grooming and had failed to prevent fatalities. The impetus may have been his father's accident, but it was more likely Jim Forĕt's crash late in that summer, which, they said, broke every bone in his body. It was because Forĕt lived. He was changed forever, but he lived. The boy's father had not.

This project would end accidents by giving wide berth along the curve that turned now more a soft angle than an S-curve. All along the road, ditches were set back, shoulders grew to car width, lanes expanded. The county added long, sloping berms at radii which were to more softly catch errant, night speeders, guiding them to an upgrade stop rather than catapulting them to their deaths. Whether by design or luck, the new path of the broad-shouldered road swept Mick Curtis out of the way. The watering hole was plugged for good.

The new road, too, cut yards off the Linnemaki property. It served to bring their old-fashioned garden closer to the road without moving it at all. The garden had grown smaller with the lesser need of the family, now only a couple, and could be worked by hand though they kept the tractor for haying on the back forty and hired it out on contract with Nature Boy to mow along the county roads. It was in his cutting for the county that the mother and son once more encountered Nature Boy.

Each year after his father had nearly plunged through Mick Curtis's front door, killing himself and destroying the last auto of his life, the boy—now a man—spent a week of his vacation back home. On this excursion, he and his mother were going past Chet Pelton's old resort, not to take part in the tribal gathering they knew was there, but to pick the wild strawberries that grew alongside the gravel sections of the road. They had to do their picking before the haymakers cut everything. The cutting made a mess of the high-growing berries the blades could reach and covered the deep-set ones with hay.

The boy parked off a side road. They bent in the sun, following the ruby runners along the shoulder from one berry to the next, taking care to drop each one they picked into their pint cup. They had agreed that it would be worth the effort even if they got only a half-pint each.

The day grew warm on his back. He removed his shirt. The sun felt good. They worked opposite sides and threw exclamations and comments across the road at each other. His picking became a smooth and trance-like. The berries made no sound falling atop their fellows in the cup, but he soon grew aware of another sound, droning and growing more pronounced each time he stooped to pick a new patch.

Sure, it would be the haymaker.

"Do you hear that?"

She listened to the drone. "Yes, it's a tractor."

"How is your harvest going, Mom?"

" We might be able to pick another five or ten minutes

before the mower comes."

It wasn't even that long before the tractor, an old one, clanked around the bend in the road.

The boy stood staring in wonder. He turned to his mother. "Look, it's Nature Boy."

Older to be sure, still sturdy, still stripped to the waist though now wearing store-bought shorts, still streaming now whitening hair down his sunbaked back, Nature Boy straddled the tractor seat as always, looking forward and back at once, cutting true and straight. He came within twenty feet of them, raised his blade, pulled off a bit, stopped the engine, and descended from the machine. From a box behind the seat, he brought out a galvanized pint measure, then uttered the only words the son had ever heard him speak: "I'll help."

He took to the mother's side, stooping immediately, plunking his finds in the can, picking with both hands. Nature Boy and his mother worked that side together picking fast, out-pacing him in minutes; moving down the road.

The boy slipped his shirt on and watched them over his shoulder. He thought he heard murmurs of talk, and maybe a laugh once, but they were now far off, bending to the ground, and he couldn't be sure what was said. He kept picking on his own side but had lost his rhythm and often stopped to look down the road at his mother and Nature Boy. Both reached for berries, sometimes, it seemed, the same one, in the sun and dappling breeze.

It took only those ten minutes. They returned. Her cup was full with what she had picked. What was in the man's tin measure, he offered the son, pouring out berries to top off his cup.

"We made it," she said. And stepping back looked at

them both, adding, "With a little help, of course."

They stood in the sun. His mother smiled. "Aren't they beautiful?"

Then Nature Boy was starting the tractor.

Mother and son stepped across the road as he passed, his bare back toward them, looking forward and back at what he was mowing.

The ride back to town was quiet. He waited for her to speak. She didn't. She rode with him along the new road, looking at the pines and at the occasional field.

When they came to the Linnemaki farm, he broke the silence.

"So, Nature Boy. Who is he?" He burned to know.

Brought back from her musing at the window, she stated it simply.

"Just a boy I knew."

2 *Oh, my son*

I TOLD DAVID he was just a boy I knew, but Loren had been the most gorgeous thing I had ever seen; propped up now on an elbow, he watched me dress. It wasn't the out-of-season, Florida tan, the rippled midriff, graceful curving chest and shoulders; believe it or not, it was the honest smile, was the clean way he dangled the leg freed from the tangle of sheets over the edge of the bunk, interested, not listless but loose, his foot swinging in little circles.

"You can't stay?"

It sounded more like a conclusion than a question. No, I couldn't stay in that little cabin, built by hand or no, set on land his summer earnings and thrift bought clear or no. He knew I had Jack's boys; he knew I had, such as he was, a husband, for Christ's sake. Anyway, he was leaving again soon. Still, he was beautiful, just as he'd always had been. A perfect fit.

"You know I won't."

"Come again?"

Again, it wasn't a question. It was not a plea. He did not lure; he had never wanted to possess. The two words hit me more like a welcome, less than an invitation. Prodigal.

I hooked myself. I knew I didn't have to answer.

I pulled the prickly wool of my sweater down. It chilled me, in moving me toward the cold outside, but I know I dilly-dallied not because I wanted to stay. I didn't, but, for sure, I did not want to go. The cold drive in the cold car to the cold house pressed on me like a winter grave. I belonged neither in the heat of the cabin nor in the freeze of the woods around it, nor in between. Somewhere, maybe; somewhere.

You'd think I like good-byes the way I lay my cheek on his chest, the way I circled his bare waist and stood a long minute. I don't. I don't like farewells which was why I was there in the first place. Saying "no" for more than the first time, I left. I didn't say "good-bye."

And he? He slipped away as he had told me it would happen. Truman called trump on Korea, and he went. He didn't go directly, but he boarded up the cabin tight, and they brought him to some god-forsaken spot to train with his 25th company or infantry or something. And then he was gone. I barely followed the war. It was a mess, and I was in a mess already. Jack's drinking had taken off in a more dramatic way; I was expecting David. It was a mess; the boys acted like it too.

I don't believe it was thoughts of Loren that brought me through. I had never mooned over a man, or pined either, or hoped either—there are better places to pin dreams, you bet—but I imagine knowing he was out there in the world somewhere, quiet, alert, and steady, helped, not because he would return to save the day—he was too bright for that—but simply because someone rooted in earth made it possible for me to survive rocky times.

Then there is a whole lot of centering and rooting that pregnancy brings. Even though Jack was blazing away, his brandy six-gun fully loaded at all times, and his sons were destroying things, stealing stuff, breaking into vacant houses, fighting at school, I was able to rise each morning, vomit, and go about business, steady as she goes toward the day I would "shit a watermelon," as mom described it, and start to live again. And David would be sweet; I could tell.

David, David. You were sweet. Sweet on me, sweet to be with, sweet to watch, so sweet I worked hard to keep far off anything that might sour your complexion. Maybe I worked too hard.

David's birth and infancy calmed things down. He charmed Jack, who kept right on juicing but turned brighter, more tolerable. His boys, rough as they were, doted on David. They must have seen hope, reason to straighten up, a promise for a happier home, for they buckled down in school and stopped terrorizing the neighborhood with pranks. And David turned me into a mother—sounds stupid. Of course, I had been half a one, but now I turned more to the family. Jack stopped, for a while anyway, calling me Tramp. That lasted for years.

But then, it might have been the second year we

summered at Rice Lake, David spotted Loren; I knew already that he'd returned.

"Guess who's back in town, Lucy?"

It was Helen who first taunted me with her best-friend winking voice. We played bridge once a month. She didn't wait for me to guess. She knew me better.

"Loren Larsen." She blurted out immediately.

She watched me as she lolled his name out over the line of tricks. The other two had no idea and pretended to be interested. Helen had an inkling but no firm knowledge. I just smiled and studied my hand.

"Wasn't he in Korea?" She continued yakking. "He lives out in a shack, doesn't he?"

One of the others got wind of something luscious and chimed in, "Does he, Lucy?"

"So they say, girls, so they say." I didn't glare at Helen but just steadily gazed and waited for her to stop.

In the car, David was all eyes.

There he was—Loren had let his hair grow very long—plowing Linnemaki's big garden out on the Rice Lake Road. Stripped to the waist. Florida tan. Straight back, solid but relaxed, steady. Gorgeous even at a distance. The flowing blond hair on the browned skin tantalized. Sweet.

"Who is that?"

David was forever curious; he must have been six then, seven that September. I played casual. Disinterested.

"Oh, that's Nature Boy."

"Who?"

"Just a man who tends the Linnemakis' garden. Say, have you thought about what treat I'll get you at the store?"

If casual didn't work, diversion might. He went for it. But the very next time we passed Linnemakis—thank God Jack was not with us—David perked up in his best announcer's voice. "There's Nature Boy."

Something about Loren fascinated David. He started to look for him and always called out when he was in the field, which seemed to me to be an awful lot.

"There's Nature Boy," David said. "Does he live in that house?"

"No, the Linnemakis live there."

"Well, where does he live?"

"I don't know." David was pestering. I was blushing.

"Doesn't he have a home?"

"They say he built a cabin somewhere out in the woods there." Even though I felt like telling him about that cabin, I couldn't. He was satisfied. For now.

Though David usually kept his voice down around Jack, it was only a matter of time before he broadcast his announcement. We three were on the way to join the two boys, staying at Lavinia's that week.

It was surprising that it took so many years.

"There's Nature Boy."

I just looked straight ahead, very quiet. Jack rolled his window up even though it was burning outside. He said nothing—then. The chill from Jack could have frozen July, and it sure cooled David's enthusiasm. He didn't repeat his announcement. He did not pester. We drove, as dark and cold as in an icehouse, on to Roy and Lavinia's cabin. Jack and Roy disappeared for four hours to the resort, then showed up for dinner merry and three sheets to the wind. Jack sat between his boys and played around with them at the table, rubbed their close-cut, stubbly heads, and cuffed them gently when they whined.

He ignored David and me. Of course David didn't notice, but I sure did.

"What's got into Jack?" Lavinia asked, wiping dishes.

After dinner, Jack paced. "I'm going down to Kormie's a while."

That relieved the tension, but then he said, "Come down later."

It was an order. I said I would. Roy, wise man he was, stayed behind. Lavinia looked worried.

I took my time cleaning up and putting kids to bed. We played a game of twenty questions, and Lavinia read a story. When they were asleep, I set the screen to the jamb quietly and felt my way down the stairs and onto the path leading toward the bar.

"Well, look what the cat dragged in."

I could tell Jack had gone ugly. Drunk and ugly.

"Didn't you invite me?"

"I don't remember you needing invitations much."

"What do you mean by that?"

Don't ask me why, but I played right into his game. Maybe I wanted to get it over with.

"Why don't you ask David?" Jack blew boozy words into my face.

"Why don't you leave him out of this? What the hell's wrong with you?"

He leered at me, cocking his head back and off to the side.

"Why don't ya' ask Nature Boy?"

He neighed the name like some old horse.

"So, that's what this is about. Can't you just straighten up?"

"No, it's about you, you goddamn tramp."

"You go to hell." I left my barstool. "I don't have to

listen to this shit."

"The hell you don't."

He grabbed for me, but I was out the door in a huff.

He followed me outside. I ran up the path toward Roy's yelling obscenities back at him. Wobbly as he was, he was steamed, blind, and crazy. He caught me on Lavinia's lawn, dove headlong tackling me, and I went down with a cracking sound. My arm hurt like hell.

"You sonofabitch. You broke my arm. "

"So what, you tramp."

He pushed hard on me getting up, and I couldn't help but scream. Someone yelled from the cabin door and Jack moved off. I hadn't felt pain like that since David, and wouldn't again until the surgery and radiation. Christ, it hurt. And he didn't get a scratch.

That was the night Jack rolled the Pontiac. I don't know where he was going—he had already passed the Linnemakis and Curtisses' tavern—I don't know that he knew. It was one of those spectacular crashes at the only curve on the road, one of those that seem impossible, end over end, spewing glass everywhere, spinning and rolling at the same time. That car did everything but burn. And Jack? He walked out with not a scratch. Bastard. I was the one with cracked ribs and a sprained shoulder. I wasn't even in the car.

That was the last summer we drove to the lake. The fun had gone out of it. Then again, paying for the damage cut into vacation funds. When we did visit Roy and Lavinia, we went afternoons just so the kids could swim. We didn't see Loren again, not for years.

Years do have a way of passing when you don't want to look up from what you are doing. Everyone says that. The boys were graduating and going to college. Escaping.

Even David became more independent, going places with his brothers, then with friends, then alone. The one summer he spent buzzing out to the lake with his high school friends I was thankful his hair had already turned toward brown for he tanned so deeply that year that I was scared. He hadn't mentioned Nature Boy in nearly a decade.

After my surgery, I took up golf to rehabilitate my arm and shoulder. David, then attending the university, was coming home weekends to join me. Jack would have nothing to do with it; he was too busy getting soused. So it was David and I again. It was nice, like his childhood.

I had lost muscle and a breast to the surgery, on the right side so unlike the other ladies, I couldn't slice. I couldn't yet swing back too far, and though it burned to follow through, I didn't let it show. I knew David was watching like a hawk, and I was too embarrassed or shy or secretive or stubborn to get into that with him. No, it was my battle, alone. What could anyone else do?

Nine holes and a beer were all I could handle.

I was tired. David took the keys.

He never drove fast, and I could relax. Riding, watching the pines pass made me sleepy, but I did see Loren on the tractor before David noticed. I wondered if it would be right. No. I pointed and called him out, softly.

"There's Nature Boy."

David didn't look. He sounded flat, busy driving, unaware. "He's still at it?"

He was still at it. Still gorgeous. What would he want with a one-breasted woman now? Maybe he wouldn't be horrified at my lopsided chest and scar. Maybe he wouldn't shudder and look away like Jack did, even dead drunk. I thought of the cabin. The warmth and calm of the cabin washed hate and Jack away.

"Yes, he's still at it."

The sun warmed me like Loren's brown, lavish chest a long time back. I flushed with sleep.

Just when you think you've got your life straightened out, it hits you hard. Even if you've been expecting something to happen, when it does, it shocks you. It seems odd, like something happening to another person instead of to yourself. I honestly don't remember if I learned about the second cancer first or about Jack's accident. I never had a chance to tell him. It happened that quick.

So I had to go through the whole thing again; alone this time, no kids, no husband. Maybe it was better for all that. I didn't tell David until the surgery was over, and though he was angry with me, I knew it was for the best. Four years had made a difference at the hospital. For all the pain, all the hurt, it still seemed easier. Do you get used to hurting all the time? Do you get used to being afraid?

At least I didn't have to take care of my basket-case husband, too. I hadn't wanted to see him dead, but I made myself look. Jack looked just like the time Spit Herbert and his goons took a dislike to him, lured him out back for a fight. He was bruised and broken, again, but for the last time. Without him this time, I came out on top. I could live again. I was maimed but alive.

David. David made it easier. The other two were like Jack and kept their distance, messing-up their own lives far enough away. But David faithfully spent a week's vacation with me each year and kept in touch between.

I warmed to summer and to my son's visits like joy

to a celebration. Spending time with one you cherish is summer in itself. I felt whole. No conflicts. Without dangers lurking at the corners. Sweet.

We were going for wild strawberries. A quarter-century melted away. We were driving the new, broad, lake road. All traces of Jack's spectacular rocket-crash had been swept away in improvements. We headed for the tribal center road where the best berries grew along the gravel shoulders. We passed close beside Linnemakis' garden once again. No one was working it now.

I've said that just when you think you've got your life straightened out it hits you hard. But sometimes hard isn't so bad. Suddenly, Loren was there.

David and I had bent over our picking for half an hour. A tractor rumbled in the distance, moving ever-closer, cutting hay along the shoulder, I supposed. We wanted to keep ahead of it, but wild strawberry picking is a slow, tedious process.

I looked over when I heard the tractor stop. By then he was slipping off the machine, bare-chested, reaching behind the seat. He brought out a small tin can and turned to David explaining in two words everything he needed to know about him.

"I'll help."

Golden, he walked through dappling shadows to my side of the road, knelt, and began picking.

I stooped beside him.

"I see you're better now," he said.

The easy smile swept away twenty-five years. He smelled like hay and strawberries.

"Neither I nor cancer could keep you down."

I laughed and fell to picking beside him. I picked what he missed. He was better for years of practice than I was, but I jabbed at his inefficiency.

"You missed a cluster here."

He brushed my shoulder and pointed.

"Look there. Going to feed those to the tractor?"

We worked together moving fast down the road. He paused, looked at me as if over sheets and pillows, shy and steady.

"He's your youngest?"

"Yes. That's David."

He picked.

Loren smiled. "He's handsome."

I wasn't going to beat around the bush. "You did well." I looked at him steadily.

We picked again.

Faster than I could imagine, he filled his pint. He guided mine to his, holding my wrist lightly, and let his fragrant berries tumble gently into my cup filling it to the rim.

We stood. Turned toward the tractor down the road. David, stooped, was watching us over his shoulder. He rose as we approached.

I held up my gleanings.

"We made it. With a little help, of course."

I stepped aside and looked up at Loren.

He reached out, took David's cup, and heaped it full.

I couldn't help but think, "Aren't they beautiful?"

Loren mounted the tractor and fired it up. He lowered the blade and returned to his cutting. Just that fast.

The ride back was quiet. I could almost hear David thinking. He waited for me to say something, but I wasn't about to open my mouth. I just rode along, watching the woods pass.

When we came to the Linnemaki farm, David broke

from thought.

"So, who is he anyway? Who is Nature Boy?"

The words fell heavily without sweetness, disturbed.

There is no way to explain away a life, so I'll let life do its own surprising, its own telling, its own hard hitting. I'm only along for the ride here, not scared to face what's coming, but, after this afternoon, I came to know that I am too scarred to go back to the past. I can't make straight what is already bent, but maybe I could help David a bit.

I turned from the window.

"His name is Loren Larsen. His family lived a mile from mine down the North Road. I knew him in school."

3 *Loren Larsen*

I NEVER WANTED MUCH. That's what I got, and I think it was almost enough. Nearly.

You make decisions pretty much on what you've seen. You learn what you like, and you try to avoid what you hate, or what scared you or, okay, what hurt you.

Lots of kids do what my kid brother did. He was the curious one. He heard the chatter of a burner expanding on the stove. He explored the sound placing his hand on the coil, and even though he snatched it away immediately, his palm looked like the rings of Saturn were printed on it. That hurt him, and it scared me. Neither of us wanted to see that again. Still, it worried Mother.

I loved my mother dearly. Thank God she wasn't a saint, but she was very good to me. I think *nourish* is the word. She nourished body, mind, and soul. She acted very calm and happy, whistling in the morning as she worked. She cooked good food. I remember the books she read to us, my brother and me. She was hardly religious, but I bet she believed in goodness. She was easy to love, so I looked for her in any girl I saw or met, and I found her out there, just once, and just a mile down the road. I didn't get that girl. I had a chance. I'm a bit slow that way, I guess.

Hurt and hate fit my father. To be fair, respect might come in there too. He was good preparation for the Army. That was for sure. He gave no quarter. He never backed down. He worked himself hard, and he worked us hard too. I learned work from him. I made my way in the world with it. Good lessons. He had me pitching gravel in the cement mixer at five years old.

I heard of a world famous mandolin player who started music at four, a novelist who started at six. What I got was manual labor. It was enough. I can listen to music or read for free anytime. Dad's hurt and hate touched me when he worked Mom over. It's okay to be hard on sons, but not on women, not on mothers. Sons get strong, tough and durable. Women get hurt. And that made me hate him. I swore I would never do that to my wife or to my kids. Never. I never got the chance to do either.

I got out at seventeen. Went into the Army. It sounds odd, but I would have stayed too except I didn't like the fighting. I hated that war. Strange, it was Mother's belief in goodness that got me through to 1954. That and work. Mom and Dad. Goodness and hard labor. Neither parent lasted beyond my return. My father died during my first hitch. If Mom had needed me then, I would have come home. But she said no. She wasn't the kind to mollycoddle or be needy. She died right before I turned civilian again.

I already had a place to come back to. I had bought twenty acres, cash, from Linnemaki who had 140, and over several Army leaves, I built a cabin in a pine grove off Otter Creek. This was just after Dad died. The footbridge and the drive connected with Antti Linnemaki's road just behind his barn. Antti had given me an easement, and I couldn't even hear the traffic passing on Rice Lake Road from my porch. It was quiet and private. Well, maybe not private enough.

Not private enough for sure. Lucy's comings and goings even when she parked up the lake road and walked in were pretty easy to detect from Antti's porch. She wasn't trying to hide, except right at the end, from her husband, Jack, though we never tried to advertise much either. We'd known each other all our lives. Our love was easy to keep up even if I was only back home from the military off and on. But then she married Jack. I couldn't understand why. That was a burn on the hand and in my heart. Still, I had been gone often and long, and I had never asked.

At first we hadn't needed privacy. We were single. Though later when we did, when she had married, if it hadn't been for old man Linnemaki putting two and two together, I would never have known I had a son of my own. Her sudden marriage early that year, her night visits when I came home on leave, my call to the war, and her baby added up in Linnemaki's mind, and he didn't wait too long to mention it to me. After I left the service, Lucy and I talked once. She had committed to her new family. I swallowed my pain. She hadn't broken ranks. I had.

She'd been married nearly two years, and the boy was already one when she stopped by two months after my return. I was working Linnemaki's big garden. She pulled out of sight round the barn, and I walked back to meet her at the edge of the field far from the road.

"I wanted to come sooner, but I really didn't think it was wise to drive right out here and announce it all. First, I didn't want you to think I wanted something from you." She thought a moment, smiled, "Other than you."

Lucy looked at the road. "Then, Jack watched me like a hawk as soon as Helen blabbed about you being home."

The man kept his jealousy in check for a long while. Not many, including Jack, were anywhere near certain. And the fewer the better as far as David was concerned. It wouldn't have been fair to him.

She put a finger to my bare chest. "But it was fun making him. Huh?"

I never argued with Lucy. "Yes. You're right." I didn't know what to say. "I don't expect I'll meet him. That wouldn't be good."

"No, it wouldn't be. Your knowing is enough. David doesn't need to know."

She went for the car, stopping at the corner of the barn, "I like you letting your hair grow. Keep it long."

That was the time we talked. It was the only time we met. Out of my sight, she would nourish our son, guard and protect him. It seemed right and good to me. Bad as Jack was, he and his two sons and David made more than enough family for Lucy. I didn't want to be the one to mess it up. I'd done enough.

But David and I did meet, finally, and before that we saw each other, not close up, just passing on the road. Those times, passing, he seemed interested. But I kept my faith with Lucy. I didn't even look up.

After the Army, I worked Linnemakis' big garden, cut hay with the tractor, and did a lot of contract work for neighbors and later for the county. I led a pretty quiet life out here. I found plenty to do. And every once in a while

I would see my son, David, go by. He would look, always; he would look real hard. I felt that meant something.

The first time, Lucy was driving that tomato-soup-and-cracker-colored Pontiac into town, so they must have been staying over at Pelton's Resort. Linnemakis' stood on the going-to-town side. I recognized the car, the only one like it around, slowing for the curve. Here's this towhead kid looking for everything like my little brother hanging out the window just staring out at me. He turned around in the seat and kept looking back until they took the curve and disappeared. I nearly fell off the tractor. But I worked hard not to look. That wouldn't've been right.

I must have missed a lot of their passing. I worked the back forty and other places quite a bit. But over the years, David and I got to know one another after a fashion. Then one time Jack was driving. I had just made the turn at the furrow fronting the road, when there they were, David pointing and talking. Lucy stared straight ahead, and Jack glowered out the window he was quickly rolling up. I felt like waving. I'm really glad I didn't.

It was almost bedtime that same night when I heard a car round Linnemaki's barn. This often happened when someone was lost. They usually turn around at the bridge and leave. This car stopped. It didn't turn around. I went out.

The headlights flashed the tractor parked near the bridge, then dimmed. Whoever it was seemed hesitant. Then the car did turn around, but it stopped. The lights went out. I don't get many visitors, day or night, so I crossed the bridge. I saw it was Jack.

I stood at the bridge. "Can I help you?"

We didn't really know each other.

When he didn't respond, I tried again. "Are you lost?"

"No, 'm naw lost. And yeah, y'can help me."

He staggered a bit out of the car, leaving the door open, and came closer.

I stood, ready for anything. "How's that?"

"Y'can leave my goddamned wife alone, that's what."

I watched him carefully. Suddenly I was back in the war. I stood stock-still.

He waved a loose arm in the air, lurching forward. "Wha'd'ya' got to say ta that? Huh?"

"I think you're drunk and don't know what you're talking about."

"So, tha's wha' ya' think?"

He lunged at me. I stepped to the side. He went down on his hands. He was getting up. "Stand still so I kin hit ya', I'll kill ya'."

He tried again. He didn't have a chance. He was that drunk.

He was hunched down pointing at me. "Lissen. You go near my wife again, I'll come back an' kill ya'—unnerstan'?"

I didn't say a word. He slumped back to the car brushing his hands.

"You shouldn't be driving in your shape. Sit in your car and sleep it off."

"Mine' yer own bizness. 'm fine."

He got into the car and weaved off down the drive. Nearly hit the barn. I saw the lights again, sweeping right and left as he negotiated Linnemaki's drive and turned toward town.

I didn't hear the crash from the cabin, but I figured there was a bad one when all the sirens sounded about forty minutes later. I didn't want to think about it or hope or anything. I wondered about Lucy and about David.

Later I heard Jack walked away from the wreck without a scratch.

Neither Lucy nor Jack drove by after that; they must have given up on the lake. Prior to Jack's visit and accident, I hadn't let myself react, not even inside. No waving. No wanting to wave. I stayed calm, not hard. Just steady. Afterward, I had nothng to react to, but at least I'd seen David grow up by fits and starts.

In later years, he would go by to the lake in a car with friends, sometimes in a car full of girls going back toward town. Once I saw him walking past, having hitchhiked, I suppose. It's seven miles to town. I had heard he was friends with my neighbor's kid, Duane, up the road. In winter, David could have seen my cabin from La Rue's back porch, if he was there and had looked for it. But summer was when I saw him more. His hair had turned darker like Lucy's, but he was brown as a berry, still looking for all like my brother. He didn't look or point any more though. Teenagers don't do that. I didn't let on.

It was Aune, Linnemaki's wife, who told me about Lucy. She had had the same thing, cancer, and lived through it.

Aune said, "She's got a chance. You know Lucy is strong." I hadn't wanted to snoop, but Aune knew I worried. She kept me informed. It was a small town.

And of course I heard about Jack's exploits too. But he never came again. I guess he didn't need to. I hadn't seen Lucy even from far off for years.

But then Jalmar's golf course out toward the lake got popular, and I saw Lucy going out with Helen on Ladies' Day. Aune thought it was therapy for her. I kept my head down. She did pretty much the same except once, with

David driving now. She looked straight at me, going to town, and I looked right at her. David kept his eyes on the road.

I imagined she was all cut to pieces under her blouse, but that did not matter. After all those years I was still looking for the same thing, someone who believed in goodness. What had gone on in the cabin between sheets was just that, between the sheets.

Then behind the wheel for the last time, Jack killed himself. Lucy was back on the operating table again, something that scared Aune, I know. Linnemaki told me about it. He said that Aune felt better after Lucy was around town once again, in a short space this time. Gave her hope even if the worst happened to her. In a way I was proud of Lucy and happy with her for surviving, twice, and giving hope to others. I thought that was something worth doing. Both Linnimakis sure appreciated it.

Maybe their good feeling led me to do something I wouldn't have done without it. I can't be sure.

Anyway, I was cutting for the county out on the Tribal Council Road when I recognized Lucy's car parked just off the road on a cabin turnout. Sure enough a little up the road, I saw them picking, had to be wild strawberries. I couldn't cut past them and spoil their picking. And since I was cutting on contract, I could stop anytime I wanted to. I don't know, but I was off that tractor in a shot—didn't even bother putting on my shirt—reached behind the seat where I keep tins for my own foraging.

David was picking, and I walked up to him. The situation seemed clear.

"I'll help," I said pointing to the other side of the road.

I crossed right over to where Lucy was kneeling. I didn't want her to think I was introducing myself to

David now that Jack was gone. I just knelt down by her and started in. I got that far and didn't know what else to do.

She moved in beside me. She always made it easy. She looked good. She looked very good to me.

"I see you're better now." I couldn't help but smile. I was glad. "I could never keep you down. Neither can that cancer."

She laughed and tried to keep up with me. I had learned to be a two-handed picker long before. Just move the can along with you. You don't have to hold it all the time. I left her a few berries, and we joked about it. I had her laughing in no time.

I touched her shoulder. It got more serious then. "He's the youngest?"

I knew it was David, but I thought it best not to let her know I'd been watching all those years.

"Yes. That's David."

I didn't think. I just burst out. "He's handsome."

Twenty-five years fled. We were back at the cabin. She had eyed me that way then, too, saying in a look, "I want to stay but I'm not going to." Now, she looked down at our hands stained with berries, reached and lightly touched mine. "You did well."

Then we just picked. Finished, I topped her tin up with what I had gleaned and stood. David was and had been watching us. It was time. We approached him together.

Lucy held up her heaping tin to David who was standing now like he expected something to happen.

"We made it," was all she said and looked at me. "With a little help, of course."

I just took David's tin and filled it from my own. Left

it in his hand. We stood there for a second or two.

Then, Lucy said, "Aren't they beautiful." I was sure she meant the berries.

I mounted the tractor and got it started, lowered the blade and put it in gear. They moved to the other shoulder and watched as I passed. I paid attention to my work, trying not to look back.

When the car turned around and stopped in the drive that evening, I knew it was David. So I came out to the bridge.

He closed the car door carefully and stood, thinking, I supposed. Then he walked up, looking troubled and surprised. "I've never seen you in a shirt before."

It was true and I had to laugh. "I do own a few. Come in handy in winter."

He swept some gravel away with a foot. "Can I ask you something? Personal?"

"Nothing's too personal here."

He had a hard time getting it out. "How do you know my mother? She never told me before today."

This was a time that going slow was good. "What's she been saying?"

His look was steady. "Only your real name. You lived up on the North Road near her. She said you went to school together."

"My real name?"

"I thought you were Nature Boy."

Though I had always hated the name, I laughed. Still, I wore little during summer and left my hair grow long. "I guess I earned it, all right. Actually, I'm Loren."

I stepped off the bridge and extended my hand. And David took it for a shake. His was smooth and strong, warm.

I kept to known facts. "We grew up together, went to school together, too, and I think we were good friends. I always have had the highest regard for your mother. She is a great woman, one to look after." I stopped there.

"After today, I was wondering."

"Nothing more to wonder."

He seemed unsure. I could tell he wanted more. "It's been a lot of years. And, yes, at one time I was, well, sweet on your mother. I'd like to think the feeling was mutual. But I missed my chance. I'm a bit slow that way. After she married Jack, your father I mean, I had to let that go."

I stopped flat in my lie. If he wasn't satisfied, even after coming all the way out here, he could ask no more.

Finally he stepped to the car. Before getting in, he looked back in a curious and admiring way. "Thanks for the strawberries today." He got in, started the car, and pulled out.

This time I waved.

Wolf Lake

ROBERT ROBBINS KICKED A STONE from the path, tugged on the brim of his Rescue Low Lake hat against the brightness of the southeastern sun, shining through a high Fall haze. He strode up onto the shoulder of the lake road and turned toward town.

He addressed the stone. "They've got more than that coming to them. Developers!"

His talk and his land were what all the hush was about when he came into the café. He was used to that.

These days he spoke his thoughts aloud but was careful to avoid being caught at it. The last thing he needed right now was to be caught talking to himself.

He intoned his best busybody, civic-pride voice, "Oh. He's just old and crazy. Been alone too long. Talks a lone, blue streak."

That's what they'd say, he thought. Probably were saying.

He shook his head, zipped the corduroy jacket against the October wind. The flotilla of gathering flocks bobbed on the choppy gray overcast lake, each duck tucking its bill to his wing.

The previous spring, skies had grown unusually clear and still. The canvasbacks, buffleheads and mallards returned in small groups, sometimes in pairs moving north to breed. He'd knelt in the reeds lining the shore, watching a pair feeding twenty feet out, one taking a turn at lookout, the other diving. Like most ducks, the male was the colorful one, holding his white hooded head high watching for predators. Always proud. Maybe too proud.

On shore, the prints left behind in the mud were likely mallard. He'd poked a finger in the center of one of them as if to determine the weight of the bird. "Too large for buffleheads."

He stirred the mud a little, leaving a pock in the center of the web. "Like Thomas reassuring himself," he said. He had earned that name, Thomas, though no one called him by it to his face. "Tommy-always-wondering. Forever-doubting-Tommy." He had heard them saying it when coming onto or passing them. He smoothed the print. "Well, that's old news."

The bufflehead pair had dived, resurfaced further out, both now on lookout. He gazed around for the fox or weasel. He saw the reeds rustling down the shore. "Fox." Too high for a weasel. He straightened, rising gingerly. The ducks again dove in tandem, sending two ringlets to the point of his reedy bar.

Years ago, this had been his favorite refuge. One spring he'd come there often. This year, when winter finally broke, he'd received his news—it hadn't been news to him; he had known, suspected for a good while—and he renewed his vigils. It had been the place he prayed. But it was not prayer now, more like meditation, thinking, wondering. He called it Occam's Point. It was there that he had simplified his life, shed the cloak of his childhood hero, Brigham Young, and had begun his struggles first with "Thomas-sayers" in school and town and eventually with his mother and, then, himself. He had won most battles. He told himself he had.

He watched the fox move toward the creek. It was a

spirit fox, invisible except for the ghostly riffling of the grass. "Same one comes around the ranch house. Must have followed the creek down."

That was his restoration of faith, nature. It was believable, sure and simple. When he had first doubted —how early did those thoughts come? At five? Eight?— he turned to the Point, to solitude. He was talking with God at that time, or maybe only to himself. He wavered. The story was too fantastic, the faith too fraught with rigor, the society too strident and close. From the Point, the lake spread for miles: open, free, expansive, certain. Eventually, the out-of-doors became his religion, untested, but he knew it must be true.

Years ago, it had been at the Point, his father found him—after hours of wondering when the horses would be fed—came down the creek, and stooped with him amongst the reeds, watching the lake.

His father had the patience of Job. Solid and kind, he had raised Robby to be independent. He broke off a reed and chewed it a bit. "I fed the horses," he finally said. "What are you doing out here, Robby?"

"Sorry, Dad. I have been praying, I guess."

"What about?"

"Asking for guidance, I suppose."

"Something's troubling you. It must be if you forgot Daisy and Pal."

He looked steadily at his father. "I did not forget. I knew you would tend them."

His father smiled, "I raised you to know that, yes."

They squatted together watching the ripples glint golden in that late afternoon. A heron lifted from the shore, stroking its way over the water, losing itself in the sun.

"Dad, have you ever worried about losing your faith? I mean in the Church."

His father stirred the air with his reed moving his jaw side to side. Finally, he looked at his son, "Robby, faith is bigger than the Church. It is like the air over the lake: it may be wet, frigid, or dry and burning, but you can't really lose it." He arced his arm out toward the shining lake, the shimmering sky.

He imagined his father as Brigham, sweeping his arm over the Great Salt Plain, opening a land to his people, a land in which they could be themselves and prosper. From that day on, he took his father's gesture as an invitation to explore the limits of his faith.

He held vigil at the Point. He kept his search private, but others, classmates, even Lloyd, his neighbor and best friend, could sense a distance, a separation, like their ranches divided by the creek, but from inside himself it seemed a gorge, wide, deep and dangerous. He doubted. And when the time came and then passed for his service, he demurred. His mother fretted, encouraged, hoped. His father silently supported his son's searching. His friends, except Lloyd, called him "Thomas," the doubter. Nearly all held out hope until he married outside the Church, made an irrevocable break, not with the community—he was part of that and brought his bride to the town, to the ranch—but with what he thought of as the impious provincialism of a faith blind to its own foibles. And finally, now, this, his latter day disease and dissolution.

His news had rocked him, much because Ginny had already left the ranch and, to a great extent, his daily life, but also because those old questions answered at the Point long before now floated up again, like the gathering

Fall flocks from the north.

He shook his head, patted his jacket pocket for assurance. It was all in the papers. He felt as shrewd as old Brigham had been. They didn't see it coming; he knew that. They thought his preacher, Martin, was a flash in the pan, an itinerant, an aberration born of "Robby's doubt."

He turned his leathery, lean face to look over Swan Creek as he passed. It ran silvery, pure, and cold this time of year down to the lake. Ran two miles from the homestead twisting all along his place forming the boundary of his and Lloyd's ranch.

The water looked crystal-gray even in the sunlight. It would freeze over soon.

The lakeshore to this point was open and clear. Because of whom? He thought. He'd kept undeveloped on up to Low Lake and the state line.

He instinctively looked behind him, then, spoke. "That stretch in town, too, that's me, too, and it'll stay open to all no matter what shenanigans they try to pull. That plot is what they're really after, at least for now."

He looked to the strange, turquoise lake waters stretching seven miles against the easterly blow that churned them up against the sandy shore.

"That's what I am, abrasive wind on big, wide waters. I'm making the going choppy. They think themselves powerful, but a headwind finds its way around."

I may have to do it alone like that wind. He did not yet dare to speak his thought. His last meeting with Lloyd left him wondering if after fifty-five years he could count even on his best friend.

"Hell, no. You can't count on that bastard. He'll just sit back and enjoy himself. As good a neighbor as he's been, you'll have to go it alone." Ginny might be different, but strong as she is, she is only human. He hoped he was wrong.

He thought about that last meeting with Lloyd.

Lloyd sat back. The leather of the chair creaked when he reclined, his feet on the desk corner. Lloyd liked that short-back judge's chair because he always wore his Stetson inside. Even at the bank. But they had never met at the bank; like now, they always talked at Lloyd's ranch, which adjoined his own at the south end, in the old bunkhouse that was the banker's hideout and private office. He had a fire going in the Franklin stove which was all it took to toast the single room, and the firelight flickered on the glass eyes of elk, deer and bear mounted above the two men. Lloyd left the fine carpets for the bank office and here covered the waxed pine boards with a few skins and the cheaper weaves he'd picked up in Mexico. He took his feet off the desk and leaned forward, elbows splayed on the blotting pad. "You know how valuable that plot is. And you know how much they want it."

"Sure."

"So, why not just turn it loose?"

"It's clear and I want to keep it that way."

"Clear! Yes, what a pretty view for all the passersby!"

"It is more than a view, Lloyd. It is an inspiration."

"But for Young's sake, Robby, why? You won't . . . you don't need it."

Lloyd bit the inside of his lip at the "won't."

Robby ignored the gaffe.

"Need nor want. That isn't the point. How long you known me?"

"For pity's sake, you know it's been better'n sixty years."

"And we have been friends all of fifty-five. Right? And you don't know me yet?"

"This isn't deer hunting or cutthroat fishing either. We're not boys again. This is common sense business, and you can't seem to get that right. Ginny . . ."

Robert started at his wife's name from Lloyd's lips. "Ginny what? What is she saying?"

"Not much. She is waiting like the rest of us. Waiting for your next move."

"Well, let that alone, then. I will be talking with Ginny."

"Don't ya think you better get to it then?"

Lloyd sighed, raised and rolled his meaty brow under the Stetson brim, and then spoke softly, "How was the walk over?"

Robert Robbins had, as he had since he and Lloyd were teens exploring the western mountains together, walked the four miles between ranch houses. Light or pitch dark, he could feel the path six decades old and more started first by their fathers even before Lloyd's dad had married.

"The walk is about the same."

"No troubles?"

"I can still manage, if that's what you mean."

"You know what I mean," Lloyd said. "I care."

"It was fine."

Lloyd turned banker-serious again, "Listen, Robert, you're gonna lose that property one way or 'nother. Why not make som'n on it even if you don't need it? They're not gonna stand for anything less."

Robert rose and put his hat on. "I'll be getting back. The moon has risen."

They neared each other, crossed their right arms to

each other's shoulder in unison. Robert's dark, sensitive eyes rested on Lloyd's jowly face, steady and soft.

"See you at the meeting, Tuesday."

Lloyd looked to his boots, "Ya, then, next week."

Robby tipped his hat at the door then closed it lightly. Outside, the crisp air glowed silver with moonlight. His breath clouded the silhouettes of twigs as he watched the old moon rise free of the mountain.

"It is as changeable as water, but always rises just the same. Regular."

No, Lloyd could not be counted on; not without coaxing, that was clear. But he was right too, on many counts. The principles of business dictated he sell. It would be good for every one. And Lloyd's devotion to business was correct; he believed in something bigger than himself. No, he didn't need the land, the money, nothing but certainty, the knowledge, at the end, that he had given, or allowed, open, free, expanse, like old B. Y. had, for the people to wonder on; as for himself, he had and would have, soon, no use for any of it.

But, then, neither did Brigham Young when he sent his folks to the lake; he just wanted to be sure no one else got it, that was all. Just to be sure. The argument seemed sound.

Well, his role was not much different, though he did not talk to anyone about it besides the preacher he'd brought in to manage the land, not even to Ginny, and certainly not Lloyd, not yet. It had to be done right. He and old B.Y., and Preacher Martin who had come up from the south, would be the only ones. The preacher wasn't a problem. But he had to tell Ginny something and was not sure of it at all.

The lake road curved sharply following the shore at a distance. A fence followed the curve now, capped, brick pilasters connected by square tubular steel rails and balusters. He ran a hand across the pickets. "Pretty darn fancy for a campground," he said aloud.

He stuffed his fists into the corduroy's pockets. "That's what burns me up," he complained to himself. "They can't leave it. Have to make it complicated, controlled, crass. Owning it is not enough. They just have to keep people out. Cordon off the lake. Well, at least you can still see it through the fence. Advertising, I suppose."

He kicked a few pieces of gravel, winced and came up short, stood breathing steadily and slowly. The pain passed. He started again, then, passing the campground entry, a large, brick kiosk set in the middle of a broad drive clearly signaling a stop. He'd questioned that blockhouse. "What is the sense in having a campground if you don't let campers come in? Members Only? Doesn't even say that. What about traveling through? Wanting to stop? Having to stop? It is bad enough that you have to pay, but resting at any price is better than being sent on your way for not belonging to the club."

He had once said that to the campground host, Charlie.

Robert had sought him out down by the dock where Charlie had been moving boats out of the water for winter storage. Charlie slid down from the red tractor seat, sensing he wanted to talk. They exchanged greetings.

Then Robert had said, "Let me ask you, Charlie, why not make, twenty extra dollars or so and let some poor, worn-out driver or, maybe, just someone who wants to enjoy the lake for a day stay overnight? You never fill up, even on holidays in summer."

"It wouldn't be fair to our members," Charlie said.

"Fair? There is a lot of humanity out there to be fair to."

"I owe it to the members first. They wouldn't expect trouble."

"Trouble?"

"Yeah. With outsiders. You know."

"No, I don't know"

Eventually he had turned on his heel and walked off. Ginny heard about his words that very day, of course.

She took his hands in hers looking into his dark, soft eyes, "It's not like you, Robby.

"I understand. But is it any good talking with Charlie about it?"

He seldom had anything to say to her warm tones and gentle arguments. She was not someone to oppose. She was usually right and always just.

It wasn't just the campground.

It was the condominium complex. Same idea. Members only.

"There you can't even see the lake. Three stories blocking the view. Cute. If you can own it. Same idea, but bigger, nastier, emptier, and more costly."

It was the campground, the condo club, and, more, the twelve food stands that each claimed to sell the best raspberry shake, the best raspberry pie, the best raspberry yogurt. Those were all the same, touting fresh raspberry this and that. Some had lines out front, always; the less fortunate closed early.

It was the pizzerias. Just like the shake-stands. Too many, and it seemed as if people could or should not eat anything except pizza and raspberry something. Not in this town.

It was the ranchettes, as they called them. Cuter than cute. Standing each alone, dotting the rise west of the lake road. "Like flies on a carcass."

It will not do. It just will not do.

Development was not new. The lake, though natural, was still forced to act as a reservoir. Water from the river that geological uplift diverted millennia back was pumped through Low Lake back up to Wolf, deepening it in spring and spilling the water loose again as the summer and fall crops needed it. Even though he would have restored Low and stopped the pumping, not much could be done with governmental and local inertia. It had been nearly a hundred years.

"Too much history for changing that. But no private anything, pizzerias, or raspberry shake stands on this land." He thought of Occam's Point and the stillness of sunrise there.

He had now walked past the bank, past three cafés that called out raspberry pie, and past the lone city park, a narrow affair split by the dirt road to the only public access within the town's side of the lake. A sign there read "Caution Mud" which did not keep boat trailers and SUVs from sinking axle deep when they backed in too far. The sign was the city's joke on strangers.

Wide swaths of blue spruce separated Ginny's house from the public landing on one side and from his prized property which marked the town's lakefront center on the other. The quiet of the pines was notable. He turned up the ramps sequestered by the cedars he had planted for Ginny. She was more comfortable wheeling up to the door without the whole town across the road watching. At the top, he stopped before the ample doors of her house.

He removed his shoes and entered.

She looked up at him, smiling. "You don't have to do that."

"Yes, I do. This is your place."

He bent awkwardly, placing his hands on her chair arms, and brushed her cheek with his lips, taking in the softness of her hair and the breath of lilacs, an old fashioned love of hers. The scent drove deep into his narrow nostrils, dizzying him for a moment. He carefully straightened up.

"I do not have to say it, but you look lovely today."

"No, you don't have to say it. But thanks. Come in. Come in."

She wheeled around, leading him to the low table where coffee had been set out. She poured and pushed the milk and sugar toward him, crossed her little hands on the table. He did not want to start.

"Robby, you walked."

"I walked, yes."

"Everything all right?"

"Fine."

"Any pain?"

"No. No pain. I am still up to it as long as I do not kick at stones."

"Six miles."

"Yes, six miles, every day but Sunday for over five years. And I am still up to it."

"Well."

He stirred the milk. He did not want to start. "You will be at the meeting?"

"Yes. Lloyd thought it would be a good idea."

"It is fine, but not necessary."

"Not necessary, but fine. I will be there. I want to be there."

He touched his jacket pocket lightly.

"You have something?" She said.

"I do."

She was smiling. "Well, what might it be, Robby?"

She always liked a surprise.

"Something I want you to have. I do not think you will like it."

"Never gave me anything I didn't love. This house? This lot? All those years? Never anything I didn't love."

"It's the ranch." He let his eyes rest on hers. "I know you will not live there anymore, I know it is too far out. But I want you to have it for your lifetime. I will be staying up there, but I have already transferred the title. I want you to have it now. Later, it will revert to the trust I have created."

He drew an envelope from his corduroy jacket, checked the seal, and pushed it to her. Her eyes were steady on his.

"I suppose asking why now would be futile."

"It would." He sighed, wavered. "I guess I wanted to see your reaction."

She fondled the envelope. Turned it over twice. Patted it. "You know I love that land."

"Seemed like."

She was smiling. "Seems like. Yes."

They talked ranch. They talked shoreline, the stretch in town and the larger piece north of Occam's Point running to the border. They did not talk Lloyd or business.

"Are you sure?" She wondered.

"No. I am the same Thomas as always. But I cannot put my finger in His palm this time. I have to go on faith."

She tapped the envelope. "This looks like more than faith."

"They built the temple on faith, yet it is hard stone too."

She nodded. She understood.

He brushed her cheek again, saw her to the lift up stairs, and let himself out. He stooped to tie his shoes and found lilac clinging to his collar and coat sleeves. Straightening gingerly, he shushed a groan and tramped down the ramp. The preacher would be waiting.

He found Preacher Martin outside the hall, looking for him. He nodded, touching the brim of his Low Laker.

"Show me."

"This way, sir."

Martin took him down the slope in the direction of the lake and around a cedar copse to a flat, level stretch that, past a new stone wall, dropped to the shore.

At the four corners of this new cemetery, Martin had placed headstones over four new oblong mounds. This he had done just in the last few hours. The bodies had come from a plot in the south.

Martin showed him where he had turned the turf in a neat rectangle, at ready in the center of the lot.

"This is it."

"It will do just fine."

Robert Robbins reached inside his jacket, handed Martin a sealed packet. "It is all ready; everything is finished. A copy of your contract is there, too. All signed."

"Thank you, sir."

"How many are coming to meeting regularly?"

"About twenty-five. Twenty-two."

"That will be enough, more will come. The quarters suit you and Malia, I trust."

"They are wonderful. We love it here. It is so open and free."

"Good. The interments were done quietly, I know."

"Yes, within two hours. Just as you asked. No one has inquired about them."

"Good. The next one will draw a crowd. I will leave that to you."

They shook hands.

"Goodbye, Preacher."

On Tuesday, he walked along the road a good five minutes without looking at the property.

Once past the southern spruce divider, he pulled down the cap.

"I do not want to see another pizzeria as long as . . . as I live."

He walked fast now toward City Hall as if to outpace the doubts that had trailed him since childhood. Once in the tiny marbled rotunda, he strode past the elevator and climbed the stair, slowly and carefully. He did not want to be out of breath when he arrived.

The council chamber hushed as he entered. He could feel the prickly gazes. Lloyd sat at the left, grinning just as he had predicted. The rest were somber ranchers, steadfast civic supporters, stolid businessmen. Ginny had parked next to Lloyd. He could not tell whether she had told his friend anything. He was happy she was there. Her eyes were steady, waiting.

He remained standing. The murmuring ceased.

"Thank you, gentlemen, for assembling to hear my

answer to your most kind offer."

Some muttered at the sardonic tone. Like old B. Y., he felt he held the important cards, cards he dealt out in a serious, earnest voice.

"When our progenitors arrived here 150 years ago at the bidding of Brigham Young, it was, more or less, to keep the gentile world out. He wanted the land kept as he saw it. This is no different."

Grumbling.

"First, I have deeded for her lifetime Swan Creek Ranch to Mrs. Robbins here. It is not for sale."

Ginny gave a single nod. The grumbling rose in pitch.

"The shore land in town is"—he waited a sliver of a minute, for a hush—"now under the direction of Reverend Martin and his Apostolic Church of St. Thomas congregation, to remain in trust in perpetuity as it is today set aside for the Cemetery of St. Thomas, established there as we meet here this morning. The state registration is here for you to examine . . ." A turbulent muttering now grew to a roar, "and the north shore property"—he had to speak louder now—"is become church camp property, open to the citizenry and visitors alike.

"As I am now fully divested of properties and rights of ownership, questions should be brought before the new church board or my designated trustee, Lloyd Baker, should he accept the position. I leave you copies of the church charter and trust."

Through the cacophony of the town's foremost business leaders, he watched Lloyd and Ginny as he set the cemetery registration and church charter and trust on the table.

Lloyd was, predictably, giving his jowl-ish laugh, shaking his sides at the spectacle as if to say, "Well, well,

Robby finally turned the tables on me;" Ginny's soft, steady gaze of understanding told him. She was glad his doubts had passed.

He enjoyed his triumphant moment but without lingering. As he left, he placed a hand each on Lloyd's and Ginny's shoulders, "I have faith in you both. I will leave you to it."

Outside again, he turned north on the road walking slowly now, lightly away from the town. The wind had shifted to the north since morning and stung his nostrils. Occam's Point lay low and faint in the distance. Off toward Low Lake and Idaho, late-leaving ganders lifted to the crisp, whitening sky, squawking and honking directions and insults at each other as they swung an arc around southward.

He did not think to mouth the words the sights, the wind, and the flight of geese brought forth:

It will be tonight. By midnight, a crisp coat of ice will quiet the lapping on the ponds and even still the soft babbling round the bends in the creek. It will be the first, hard freeze.

The Open Road

THE "OPEN ROAD" IS usually interpreted to mean free with wide, far horizons, plenty of room. Another reading of the phrase indicates that when traveling on the highway you "open" yourself to whatever the "road" will bring. Most guard against this. The few accept it as the price of traveling. Here an illustration of both definitions and good reasons to guard and to accept:

I do love the early desert dawn. The air is still cool from the night but wears a thin coat, unbuttoned, which tells of the heat to come. It will be sunny, always. That sun and incipient warmth bring me out of the Westfalia to cook my breakfast at a picnic table of this Nevada interstate rest stop.

The Silver State allows an eighteen-hour layover here, provides tables on concrete pads or on grassy lawns. My yoga mat on concrete beats an uneven desert floor, but I do prefer lawn for both yoga and weight training, which I do while breakfast simmers on the Coleman stove.

I-80 roars its constant commerce out toward rolling, brown stone-studded hills and further to the mountains north of here. The grind of sixteen-wheelers flattens over the scrubby desert weed and baked, cracked mud scrolling to the south of the rest-stop oasis.

At my lone picnic table, I combine my meal-making with morning exercise routines—at home alone, nude— here, on the open road, especially in the Nevada morning, clothed, but in as little as possible. To avoid concern over my odd-looking sun salutations and scant clothing, I choose the most remote, isolated rest spot I can find.

On August 25, 2011, I parked in the very first slot afforded to cars, the one farthest from the *wunder hus* (its toilets) to which travelers hurry, bilious birds flying from their nests, and from which they meander, geese strolling on a park lawn, content. Average visiting time, I can't help but notice: two minutes. Forty yards away, I dawdle over luxurious oatmeal preparations and stretch patiently, slowly, toward my coming day of travel.

Far from the central stream of highway life, lounging over my bowl of oats in the morning sun, clad in my briefest of briefs, a wayward fellow traveler surprised me. Despite ten open slots down the way, he pulled in directly beside my isolated Westfalia camper whose doors were flung wide. Striding as directly as he could round the intervening low fence and tables, he stormed my single-occupancy picnic table. His invasive greeting shook me out of my open frame of mind.

"Do you have clothes on?" He began.

My defenses, my ire, and my indignation rose, but I remained seated, stirring breakfast.

My breakfast is not invariable, but as with many things in my life, is regular, repetitive, so borders on obsessively rigid. This day, like most days, I prepared steel-cut oats, a gift from my one-time, proto-son-in-law, Smari, who worships good food. I prepare these oats with strawberries for sweetener; blueberries, providing anti-oxidation; raspberries for a fresh zest; and a little light milk to make the gruel smooth. I had been cooking oats for nearly two years as a method to measure and control starch intake. The berries render the use of crystal sugars unnecessary. Sometimes as a rare treat, I drizzle maple syrup on top. I cook oats for thirty-eight minutes, adding milk at twenty, fruit—less the raspberries—at thirty-two. I top the cooked mixture with the raspberries which, uncooked, better release their sharp flavor.

My delight in this breakfast is rooted in adolescence when Mom worked the early shift at the hospital kitchen and Dad woke me and prepared my breakfast. I did not think of his cooking much, though I know now it was a joy, something he could do for a kid of his, something anchoring and regular for his own, often chaotic life— in short, something at once physical, practical, and emotional.

The meal in those days was often rolled oats sprinkled with brown sugar. The center I dimpled with a thick pat of butter, marking the hub of the meal and then poured a ring of milk around the perimeter of the concoction. The sugar melted and darkened in variegated patterns as it dissolved into the different strata (butter, oats, milk) before my daily coup de jour, which was to cut a channel in the oat mound, allowing the liquefied butter mixed with deliquescent sugar to pour into the milk. My excavation opened a river of yellow cream that swirled into the milk ring, carrying the silt of dissolving sugar floating all around the circumference. The dynamic mixing turned breakfast into an aromatic, sweet, and rich delight at the first taste of which my body sprang to life despite the dark Minnesota mornings. You can easily see that the depth of this devotion brooks no rude interruptions.

Similarly in the tranquil desert dawn, the first bite of rich sweetness—tempered by low fat, absence of processed sugar and the flavor of chewy, granular oat bits rather than the slurry that rolled oats used to bring me—

begins my adult days. The emotional patina is the same, washing me over with warmth, with coursing nutrients and with a sweetness like the sun to a cactus flower. As an adult, I combined the buzzing lift of coffee—creamy with "spume" of partially skimmed milk rather than the hot chocolate Dad used to fix me—to ready me for challenges of the day. Ah! Breakfast! The meal that sets you free!

Yes, sets you free, if you are free to enjoy it unmolested.

But my handsome, new companion, dressed in tight-fitting, button-down shirt, striped tie, and shiny slacks, had broken the barrier. Now he rephrased his question, "Are you dressed?"

"Of course," I countered. I couldn't ignore the rudeness of the question, and so, stood up to demonstrate what he could not see below the table top, my scanty briefs.

"Pl-lease!" He crowed, cowering in faux disgust, averting his gaze, and crossing his arms before his face as if I were pelting him with my blueberries rather than exposing my naked torso and legs.

"You should wear some clothes."

I sat again and shrugged. I thought he did not need to enter my sphere. If he had to avoid the affront skin seemed to give him, he could have parked like most arrivals square on the kiosk. For his part, he was fully clothed and covered, his long sleeved shirt buttoned at the wrists, his cuffed dress pants belted firmly brushed the tops of the high polish shoes. It was 75 degrees out already, but then, he probably had air conditioning in his SUV.

"I was exercising," I told him.

"Hey"—now he was advancing again despite my unrobed state—"I just bought this car—a good deal at $2,400—and I have to get to the state line by noon."

I eyed the Ford Bronco, which looked to be worth more than he paid for it, easily capable of running the next 200 miles to Utah. I shrugged as if to indicate "so?" An early morning Silver State bee began buzzing in my brain.

Now exactly when does the thought, "Oh, here it comes," first express itself when you realize you are involved in a solicitation, not a conversation? I am much quicker on the draw answering the phone, walking the streets of the East Bay, or approaching the doors of Safeway. But I drop my guard on the open road. Was it the story-telling tone he shifted into, body language, or his advance in the face of my offensive quasi-nudity? It may have been his tightly-buttoned visage that moved me to think, "Oh, here it comes." And here it came.

He held his hands out in supplication. "I'm nearly out of gas."

It is a terrible thing, I know, to be running low on petrol in the middle of nowhere; it deflates hope and the ego at equal rates. I rose to point yonder, to the gas station across the interstate accessible through the underpass. Its yellow-and-white standard towered over the raised road.

"I know where the gas station is," he said.

I thought, "Oh, here it comes: 'I don't have any money, and I have a long way to go.'"

He echoed my thoughts. "I don't have any money, and I have a long way to go."

I must have started shaking my head before he finished, perhaps before he started. He did not look indigent or hard-luck. The obvious scenario thundered in my now-heightened consciousness: "Oh! I get it. You are in the middle of the desert, with a newly purchased vehicle which is nearly out of gas, you have no money, and must get to Utah, quick! Now how does that happen to a person like you?" My own naked body language must have tipped him to my un-altruistic intentions.

"I know it sounds odd, but that car took all of my money, and the sheriff told me I had to get to West Hanover before noon," he explained.

Now we have the police involved! I want nothing more but to wash my breakfast dishes.

He continued with explanations about licensing, his good fortune at finding the car, the color of the desert sky. I had stopped listening.

After a minute, I stood, faced him chest on. "I can't help you," I stated flatly.

Without hesitation, no doubt in the spirit of conservation of energy, he stopped yapping, turned on his heel, and headed toward the people-stream, all in one motion. I watched him go. I could see him plying the flood of humanity down at the toilets with his gibe, first a trucker, then a middle aged couple, finally, a member of his own SUV tribe. I walked to the van and shut all the doors against any casual prying he might do on his return.

I performed some moderate lifts now that my privacy had been restored. First stretch, then compress. When my only neighbor did come back to his gas-beast, I had already formulated my strategy. Indignant that this itinerant panhandler should upbraid me for scant clothing while breaking the peace of each and every traveler who had need to "rest," I set the weights on the picnic table and stood arms on my hips to inquire.

"Any luck?"

"Yeah, I earned ten bucks," he bragged. I suppose a flimflam man sees this as an honest fifteen minutes work, so *earned* had to be the right word.

Before I could return to my exercise he continued. "You know where I am from?" He asked.

"Yeah, California."

"I'm from Thousand Oaks."

"I'm from Oakland."

"How are things there?" He asked, giving me a way to end it.

"Tough." I let it drop like my twenty-pound weights.

He gaped at the word as it thudded to the ground. Again in a single motion, he turned, jumped into the Ford, started and uneconomically roared the engine. At the underpass he and sped directly up onto the highway, without giving a thought to gassing up.

The wide desert vistas opened all around me once again. My punctuated breakfast again grew still, leisurely and calm. I had opened myself to the road and mostly had kept it free. I was at liberty to finish my weight routine while the dishwater heated on the stove. Clean-up is part of breakfast.

Going Downtown

Most would have turned back
at the first bang
of the garbage can cover
or at the first sight
of the empty clothesline,
and he would have too
in another time
when the scent of pine
played wildly in his nostrils
or when the snow crust
unbroken beneath his paws
crunched or scraped.
But now a bit blind
and years since he had really
smelled the ripped flesh he ate
he ambled into town
at dawn
coming in from the west
and before he knew
they had gathered
around to see what the sheriff
would do.

It was a dangerous situation.
That, he could sniff.

Tierra Amarilla

A ROAD TRIP MUST BE TAKEN avoiding the trunk highways, certainly in the main off the Interstate so as to afford experience to flower. This can be intentional, happenstance or forced. It does seem to matter which. Sometimes, being forced to slow down or to stop altogether is the best kind of travel.

The science of pneumonology sprang to the forefront of my scant technical consciousness on Interstate 35 just seventeen miles south of my hometown of Cloquet, Minnesota, which I had driven 2,435 miles to reach. Sprang might be the wrong word here, perhaps growled, rumbled, and pounded better describe the sequence.

I had been driving a section of I-35 which seemed to be the beneficiary or victim of President Obama's American Recovery Act. It was a two lane, two way nightmare, intensifying its horror after dusk, bumpier than the gravel washboards that ran off into the Carlton County outback that surrounded me. Naturally, I thought it was the road at first. Immediately, though, the bumping became growling, grew into heavy rumbling, and, then, turned to pounding. Yikes, a flat!

I travel my usual fellow-traveler-maddening 55 miles an hour in my go-easy-on-the-engine '83 Westfalia. (I wonder if I ever recovered from Richard Nixon's cap on speed limit.) Stopping was not a problem, and even with little shoulder, close oncoming and closer passing traffic, in pitch dark now, changing the tire was a vicissitude of travel rather than an ugly challenge. A dirty job well done, I thought. But that is not pneumonology.

No, pneumonology is, or became, the study of types of flat tires over the course of a road trip, serial blow-outs, if you will, engendering in its turn a specialized branch of the science, pneumonography which is the measurement of tire sizes and profiles contributing to catastrophic failure of vulnerable air passages, or what instantly became air passages rather than air containers.

To be clear though not short, what happened south of Cloquet, Minnesota, was repeated north of Clear Lake, Iowa, and on the corner of Rio Arriba County 531 and New Mexico State Highway 89 in Tierra Amarilla: to wit, the road vibration in combination with the profile of my new, hometown-purchased tires—the only heavy-duty tire available for the Westfalia—sent the wheel covers into rotation like little clocks, the interior figure of which acted on the new, extended tire valve stems like knives in the hands of vandals. These previously decorative wheel covers, now acting like tweaked knobs of vicious egg timers, bent, sliced or unseated tire stems, allowing pressure to drop from 50 psi to zero in a second. This, added to the realizing-what-happened time and stopping time was long enough for the wheel rim to shear and shred the lining of the brand-new tire. Pneumonologically speaking, instant flat followed by total destruction.

You have the same question I did: "Where is this leading?" Ultimately—this is in the realm of psychology, not pneumonology—it led to petulance, impatience, and depression.

Petulance ensued when I called the second tire dealer

(the first being the hometown guy) to say, "I have some bad news about that replacement tire you sold me," but was greeted first with, "Ya know, I meant to call you . . . ." He meant to call. He meant to call to give me his evidence that the wheel cover was the culprit. Thank you. Thank you. Too late, thank you.

Impatience rose after a three-hour stint at the third tire dealer who changed the long stems to short ones and, disastrously, rotated one of the new tires to the front, moving the in-use spare to the right rear. I did not want to wait another day for another replacement. I had run through Iowa, Missouri, Kansas, Oklahoma, and Texas to New Mexico on this spare and would take my chances. Correction: I had run the spare, the beneficent low profile, non-rotation-inducing spare, in the right front position, the only position with enough quaver, in chain reaction, to cause a flat. Now that lovely, efficient spare was in the rear. At right front rolled a new, high profile, vibration-amplifying villain who cared little for long or short stems and who would within 94 miles prove that it is not a good idea to run your only spare tire mounted on an operating wheel.

Then deep depression descended—something like, I suppose, a dragonfly feels, wheeling freely along the highway one second and dripping down a windshield going seventy miles an hour in the opposite direction the next, minus the consciousness, of course.

Pressure? Tire pressure was not the only thing on my mind. On the southbound trip from Minnesota, I was accompanied by my older brother who flew in from San Francisco to meet me just for this ride back. We had not spent this amount of time together since adolescence, when we shared a bedroom. Did I want to impress this older sib with the wonders of Westfalia and the awesomeness of the American West? Yes, as you younger brothers know, I did. Instead I opened him to the vulnerabilities of vacationing in a van. Result? People who feel stupid grow petulant. The unintelligent wax impatient, the dumb depressed.

When I made the U-turn back toward the road we had missed in the dark, I lost the right-front, offending wheel cover, and felt, for the third time, the all too familiar pounding growl-rumble 300 feet down Rio Arriba County Road 531. My immediate self-assessment was, what kind of brother would drag his sibling on a square tire voyage to a place as desolate and empty as Tierra Amarilla, New Mexico without a spare tire? We—all because of you—are stuck.

I knew that sometimes being forced to slow down or to stop altogether is the best kind of travel, but I was not ready to accept the axiom at that hour. Disaster had struck. In a petulant, impatient, and soon to be depressed mood, I backed or rather hobbled onto a grassy strip beside a wide gravel driveway, cinched the parking brake, and sat stony still, wanting nothing but to cry or die.

The stars and planets on this clear cold night had aligned themselves against me. I deflated like my third ruined tire, bumped, thumped and slumped. I lay draped over the steering wheel, scathed on the inside, squashed on the outside. Nick, ever the vigilant attorney, aware of civil law, was worried only about in whose yard we were trespassing.

This new fear pumped me with a bit of the air of action. Whether it was to defend my impulse to get off the road or to sooth his legalistic mind, I do not know, but, lightly inspired now, I hopped over to a mail box mounted just outside the drive entry, flopped the door flap down and read, to my great relief, the name Amando Flores. I did not know any Amando Flores, but to my studied-though-halting Spanish language mind, this was a godsend, carrying a much friendlier, caring ring and more to my liking than a stern, perhaps litigious-sounding McEachren. It may sound narrow, but I have yet to meet anyone of Mexican descent who has not effused friendly, caring sentiments. And such a wonderful, soft name, Flores. Nick was not so impressed.

Never mind him for now. Re-energized, I took a nerve-calming walk back to Highway 89, looking for the missing wheel cover. Somehow, treading the path of our entry to doom lifted my psychic sidewalls and even though I did not discover the errant cover until the following morning, I returned to the listing van feeling like I could do something.

The something I did was to rifle through my books, locate my large format road atlas I had tucked away, leaf through each state looking for my American Automobile Association number I had scrawled somewhere three weeks before when California 5TFV245 would not start at high altitude. I started with W for Wyoming since it had been at Grand Teton that I called the 800 number to retrieve my member designation. The third time was a charm; fifteen states later I discovered a marginal note beginning with 1-800; following this, like a realignment of astrological bodies, was my twelve digit AAA number. Eureka! I have found it.

I had already expressed heavenly gratitude for AAA's automatic renewal when stuck in the Tetons, but my inward chords were again lifted to the skies in thanks when Laura from California took my call.

"Yes, we can help you. Are you in a safe place?"

In my mind, yes. Nick had other ideas.

While I had walked, searched, and then talked to lovely Laura, he was busy Googling Amando Flores.

We were about to get our first history and culture lesson about the town in which we were trapped. He found three Amando Floreses in the vicinity: One was an artist, noted for his photography, who was presently conducting a one-man show in Taos. The second, a County Assistant District Attorney, retired. The last, I could say later, was deceased, leaving behind, Nick told me, a wife and three children. If the artist was hosting us, it was likely to be invasion of artistic privacy. The position of the ADA was a given. The bereft, perhaps impoverished survivors of the third Amando Flores would receive any jury's sympathy. I would opt for the latter. Nick did not like any of the possibilities.

Night had fallen. Like it or not, we had to wait until morning to find out where we were, who could sell us tires, and where to go to discover when any of this could happen. The temperature at 7800 feet had dropped to 36 degrees Fahrenheit. I shivered in my dreams.

And what dreams may come when the defenses are down, when stuck a mile and a half high in the spare, flat air, when sitting, empty and friendless at the edge of somebody else's domain? Murder dreams, of course.

In my dream, when I heard the news of the child's death, I knew I had committed the crime. The details were not important though I likely used a tire iron to bludgeon the poor thing; I was guilty as charged. No doubt about it. It was only a matter of time before the DA turned his attention to me. But as I waited in the dark clouds of suspicion and remorse to be questioned and prepared myself to confess, self-preservation spoke. The wheel of justice might not, guilty as you are, discover the truth. Anything could have happened. A one-armed, itinerant artist could have struck the blow. If murder would out, well, I decided, I could plead self-defense, though how that would work seemed dubious even to this sleeping dreamer. Still in my dream, I clung to depression if not to hope.

Well before dawn, I woke depressed, startled, guilty. Relief would come. The dark feelings persisted, but at least I was certain, once fully awake, that I had not done the deed. I'm not the type.

It was 6:00 a. m. too early to call for tires. There was no need to wake my brother. I had to walk again.

This time I found the wheel cover. Hallelujah. Things were picking up. I started northern New Mexico cultural-history lesson number two that morning.

I found the town name, Tierra Amarilla, posted in the parking lot of Los Lobos Café, which was housed in a huge building, at least for this burg, painted with neat two foot high letters "T-I-R-E C-E-N-T-E-R." Things were really picking up.

Lesson two, the town name was a difficult one to pronounce at six in the morning, Tierra Amarilla. The trill on the r's, the juxtaposed a's, as well as the double l's threw me. After all, Cabrillo College on the California Coast is locally pronounced like the cleansing pad with the state abbreviation appended as a prefix. How to pronounce this town's name correctly, I couldn't find out. No locals lined up to enter Los Lobos. Though there was a light on in the café, a barking dog barred the threshold. From a safe distance, I noted the opening time, 7:00 a. m. and walked on toward the medical center in the distance.

In the pre-dawn light, everything in Tierra Amarilla appeared spread out. It is the land of plenty—plenty of land. The big building of Los Lobos is set off by itself, as is the medical center, as are the three other tire shops— all three in ruins (not the best sign)—the gas station, the school bus barn, and the school itself. Houses remote from one another dotted both sides of the highway. One two-story building poked above the trees a way off. The signs of life other than a passing highway car or two were at the medical center, where lights shone out the windows, at the gas station where a man peeked out the front door then retreated behind and shut it, and at the reticulated metal bus shed where four diesel bus engines chugged into life one at a time. The Rio Arriba Medical Center marquee flashed 38° then 6:38.

The medical center standing by itself, a five-minute walk down the drive, was lighted but closed. No luck or conversation there. As I re-crossed the highway to approach the now-warmed buses, each in its turn surged into motion, climbed toward me to the elevated road bed and turned away down Highway 89, one of them signaling at the flashing yellow semaphore which marked "my" road. Six other buses stood silent outside the barn. Someone must be at the bus building, a mechanic, perhaps.

I paused at a triangular plot of ground that directed traffic to right and left at the head of bus-barn road, where a historical placard commemorated the infamous 1968 Courthouse Occupation by the followers of Reies Tijerina[1] which started with a citizen's arrest of the district attorney and ended when the National Guard

1 . . . led a struggle in the 1960s and 1970s to restore New Mexican land grants to the descendants of their Spanish colonial and Mexican owners. https://en.wikipedia.org/w/index.php?title=Reies_Tijerina&oldid=743956577 (accessed 12/02/2016)

forced the release of hostages. History and culture lesson three. I was pleased at this land-rights business; it seemed right up my alley, or driveway.

I had more pressing business than history at the moment; I was freezing and wanted somewhere to warm out the chills. The bus shed was not far away , and I headed there. I had been right; the office off the large maintenance shop was occupied by a sturdy, youngish-looking man who looked at me with a mixture of suspicion and curiosity.

"I'm just looking to warm up a bit."

"Yes?" He seemed to want more.

"It's pretty cold out there this morning."

He agreed. "Frosted last night."

"Tim. Tim Jollymore . . ."

"Hernan. Hernan Sanchez."

He was the supervisor of the bus fleet, he told me with pride after I complimented the early start of the buses I had seen leave. I mentioned what I knew about the town. Los Lobos Café and my need for the Tire Center.

"I don't know why they keep that sign up," Hernan said. "The tire business is never open. In fact, hardly anyone goes to the café either. You might try the gas station for tires."

I asked about it and Hernan made personal the historical placard I'd seen about the events following June 5, 1967:

"My grandfather was the sheriff at the time of the Courthouse Occupation. One person was killed during that time.

"And then about a year later, someone murdered my grandfather. You can know who did it, but no one was going to do anything about it. They never arrested anyone."

His tale brought the placard to life. We were already friends.

"Say, you know Amando Flores? Lives down 531?" I asked.

His eyes danced in amusement. Through a half smile, he told me, yes, he knew him but Amando was dead.

"You parked down there?"Hernan asked.

"Not down really, on the right side of the road."

"Maria, Amando's widow, lives on the other side. Down below."

I remembered the place by a yappy little dog that had greeted my passing.

"Who lives right across the road?" I asked.

"Arturo. Arturo Morales. His son Mateo lives around in the back with his wife, Valentina."

Well, I wasn't looking forward to telling Nick but didn't know that by this time he had already found out.

Hernan and I chatted up the schools. There were 300 students in the area, at least four busloads. When he found out I had taught, he revealed that he was the football coach of the junior high team. I thought that with 300 students in the whole district it might be tough to field a football team.

"No, we have both offensive and defensive squads. Twenty-four on the team. We're 2 and 0, won last night as a matter of fact."

I was warmed by Hernan's civic and personal pride as well as the toasty office. The town was shaping up as a decent, if tire-less, place; civil rights and clean fun seemed to prevail. I wished my first Tierran friend luck with his season.

I had one more stop before returning to the van and

my brother: the gas station.

Like every place in town, it sold no tires. But I told my sad story and sat at the little table off one side of the cash register counter. I moved the store operator's, Ramon's, bowl of berries over and worked with my iPhone 4 on the blue-checked oilcloth. The warm station office was busy now with morning traffic: a mom gassing up and getting her third grader a snack, a hunter returning from a cold stand, a failing farmer buying cigarettes and ruing the lack of rain and the sudden cold. When I got no answer at the Big O store across the Colorado border, Ramon laughed.

"They don't open until 8:30 up there."

"I'll try later."

I found Nick across the way, sitting outside Los Lobos, having a morning cup, and eating the Rancher's Breakfast Roberta had cooked up.

"I'll buy you breakfast," he said. Big brothers can be wonderful.

I felt like we were snuggled before the heat register listening to *Big Jon and Sparkie*[2] on the little family radio. The fraternal care warmed me. I related my discoveries, he his.

At 5:45, before I had slipped out of the van, Valentina Morales passed down the driveway on her way to work. When she arrived just after six, she called Mateo, who at 7:00 a. m. paid Nick a visit on his way to the state highway garage.

Nick had explained how sorry we were to be imposing. We would be on our way later that day. Mateo

2 Jon Arthur Goerss, as Big Jon Arthur, was the host of the Saturday morning children's radio series *Big Jon and Sparkie, 1950-58. https://en.wikipedia.org/w/index.php?title=Jon_ Arthur&oldid=743604471 (accessed 12/02/2016)*

had not seemed impressed, Nick told me, but grunted that his parents would return from Santa Fe later that night. They were the owners.

Just as the dawn illuminated the mountains surrounding the Rio Arriba valley, our acquaintances shed light on the sights and site of the town. It was a place most passed on their way north toward Durango, but it lived and breathed history and active existence in a pretty way, each early riser taking up his bus keys, spatula, blueberry bowl, or apron and a sense of humor adding his own spice to the bowl of communal life. Those we were to meet opened like exotic flowers to the oddity of strangers, exuding the perfumes of their simple lives like heliotrope in the garden of Maria Elaina Fernandez four miles on the lake road from town. MEF told us her family history, the way to Gem Lake, a bit of her medical condition, where her sons lived and what they did, that she had visited the optometrist that morning, and about the meeting she was to attend that afternoon on the other side of the lake. She told all this in her sunny driveway during the passing of ten minutes.

In TA, the short form of the town name, pronounced as one (târ-mə-rē´-ə), we met highway workers, a bus driver-barrista, artists, Alzheimer's sufferers, European bicyclists, Bay Area rent refugees, adobe slatherers, carpenters, Korean-American drum makers, cooks, waitresses, wandering neighbors, furniture makers, too many overly-protective dogs along the roads we bicycled, historical figures, and social critics. What a way to travel! We stood still, while the town passed before us.

"The Three Ravens Coffeehouse," the sign said. Other than the corrugated metal roof and adobe walls, it looked like a transplant from 4th Street in Berkeley: hand-painted tables and chairs under the long porch eaves, a serpentine gravel path leading to the open door, beamed ceilings, divided-light windows, artwork everywhere inside, more hand-painted tables and, the tour de force La Marzocco espresso machine churning out lattes.

"Sorry, guys, it's going to be a few minutes," she said. "Ken is sick this morning and I'm doing everything myself."

"We're in no hurry." The irony was lost on her.

"Yeah, he looked really bad earlier. Especially his eyes, whew! I've got two orders to make here and I'll be with you."

The tall drink of water, named Dylan, who sauntered in the side door, noted I was looking at the bookshelves set out with china plates of the Three Ravens design.

"I made that shelf. Right next door here," he said.

He was a local.

"No nails, glue or pegs. Friction fit."

"I thought so," I said.

"This one is ply but I make a solid ash and a cherry one as well. Costs a bit more, but solid wood is worth it. I have one over at the house."

"I love ash. Built a clock case out of it years ago. I'd like to see it."

"Sure. Get your coffees and meet me next door. I'm on break. I'm helping my carpenters on the deck project."

Sally, the bus driver I'd met that morning, was working furiously over some panini and smoothies.

"Yeah, I've got to pick up my daughter at one, bring her to grandma's house, then scoot back to warm up the bus for the afternoon run when school lets out. I hope Ken can take over here. He looked pretty bad this morning."

"I met Hernan this morning," I told her.

"Yeah? Yeah. He is my boy's football coach."

"He told me about the team."

"Yeah, I can't be late picking Shea up either. I've got to keep on time."

She clattered around the small kitchen, opening and slamming fridge and cupboard doors for a few minutes, then called out the order.

"Chicken panini, two raspberry-banana smoothies." Two women appeared for the panini and smoothies.

One of them asked me, "Those your bikes out there?"

"Yes. We just finished a ride looking for the lake."

"Hmm. That's a ways, to Gem Lake," she nodded.

"Well, we never made it. We couldn't find the right turnoff."

"It's just down the hill off 531 past the school . . ."

I admitted that I'd seen the sign. On the way back.

"We ride in the mornings. Just got back from a trip across Europe," she said.

"Italy?" Nick wanted to know.

"No, we started in Rovaniemi Lappi and went through the Baltic States."

"Finland?" Now I was really interested.

"Yes."

"Our mother was Finnish."

"Oh, so you know Rovaniemi, then."

"Yeah, Santa's home, but not really. Grandma came from the islands off the Swedish east coast. Local name is *Gombiligotilibu.*"

She cut to her narrative. "It rained every day. We were supposed to go on after Prague, but it was pouring there, too."

I told them about our problems.

"Don't let them tell you you have square tires."

I should have heeded her warning.

"My dad was in the tire business," she said. Then, indicating her partner, "Some fool told her that she had square tires. Cost a fortune to fix. They just wanted to make the sale. She didn't need new tires."

Her partner nodded and seemed about to speak.

I'd been hoping to escape. "Our coffees are up," I said, masking my relief with caffeine enthusiasm.

I left my small sympathy behind and took the coffee to Dylan's, the shelf maker.

"Here's the ash . . ."

We spent the better part of the lunch hour meeting people who came to the café and the little neighborhood of the courthouse next door. A good share of the patronage came from deputies, the county court brass and managers next door—the same courthouse that forty-three years earlier had formed the center of land-rights controversy that had attracted national attention.

"I sympathized totally." Ken, who had brought his watery eyes downstairs when Sally had to leave, was talking. "Until Reies came up from Albuquerque for the fortieth anniversary."

"That must have been a big deal."

"It was, but when he started to talk shit, I stopped listening. Now, he thinks it's all the Jews who own the banks that are the problem. He sounded like a Nazi. Damn Jews this, damn Jews that . . . I just walked away."

He was making me a decaf latte. I asked for the bathroom key.

"The Outer House. That's what we call it. The only self-composting outhouse in the county. I had to fight to get that too."

He had already told the story of saving the restaurant building from the bulldozer with only a day to spare, spending scads of money and taking years to restore it.

"The State Health Department in Santa Fe told me I couldn't seat more than three people inside since I did not have a toilet. We went round on that one. How about outside? I can have tables outside. No, they weren't going to give in.

"Okay, how about this? I'll put six tables outside anyway."

They told me I would be arrested.

"Okay, how about this? I'll get the television crews up here as you handcuff me and haul me away for selling coffee. All I want to do is sell coffee."

The guy says, "You wouldn't do that, with the TV."

"Oh yes I will," I said. Ken was getting worked up here, rubbing his hands in glee. "And I'll post my blog with your picture and the story and have every coffee drinker in Rio Arriba County e-mail you and your boss, and all their relatives too. We'll string police tape around the building and wear prison jumpsuits, all orange—that shows up well on TV—and have you arrest someone who just wants to sell coffee.

"I had to have a toilet. If I put one in, he said he could approve six tables, total.

"Then the County didn't want to approve The Outer House. The plumbing would have been nearly the same, maybe a little more, but this composting outhouse is "green," and how can you say no to that? I worked on them, and they finally rolled over on it. Now they all use it! The courthouse had a water leak, lost pressure and everyone had to come over here. I made each one ask for the key."

The Outer House really was a wonder. It was a little Pantheon. Its octagon sat on a spiffy concrete pad that took decorative tile well. Inside the cedar walls shone in skylight and soft low wattage electrical sconces, a little winter heater, an original painting created especially for the space, and the high-tech composting biffy all decked out with complex directions and caveats. It did take some study, but the thing worked fine. No bureaucrat in his right mind would disapprove of a wonderful whirligig like this. I bet people came from miles around just to pee in the thing.

Ken closed at two—only a solitary disappointed caffeine junkie came by after—casting a tranquil, sunny calm on the porch where travelers could wi-fi and charge phones at the tables all hours.

Jim, a Taos-born and bred plasterer, worked quietly around the corner on the gable end of the building, restoring the original coat. He stood on his Mexican-style scaffolding: two huge A's framed in four-by-fours that each hold a short post 90 degrees to the wall. Across these posts, Jim lay his two-by-eight planking.

"I learned this in Mexico."

"And the adobe trade?"

"In Taos," he said.

He cautioned me about sweeping the deck, which I did only to kill some time.

"I'm going to be recoating over there in the next couple of days. It'll get messy fast."

"No problem, Jim. I'm just wasting the afternoon doing a good deed."

I watched him hoist a few buckets up from the wheelbarrow full of mud, then slather it on and smooth it to the wall.

"Stucco would last longer, for sure, especially on the wet side, but Ken wants to keep the authentic finish. Artist, that Ken. You know he makes those drums you see inside."

I knew. And his wife designed the Three Ravens line of tableware. That I knew since Nick had bought a couple of plates for Valentina Morales as an offering of peace and anti-trespassing medicine. They were nice. Arty. Maybe artsy. Definitely pricey.

Valentina liked them. Maybe she knew their value though I found it hard to visualize the Moraleses bending elbows on the coffee bar at the Three Ravens. They seemed homey, part of the tamale and menudo set, rather than latte-lous. *Ella era muy amable* and accepted the plates with her quiet grace. Mateo warmed up a bit after that.

"Ya, that's alfalfa there. I might get the third crop if it doesn't freeze too soon."

He pointed to the fields across the fence. He answered questions. Didn't offer much of anything.

We would meet his parents that evening. None of us, then, would have much to say; we'd all be polite and tolerant. I was not surprised. Nick was relieved.

It was as if we had been teetering on the fence rail between the coffee house and our squatter's strip, between the 'artistic' community and alfalfa growers, between those whose lineage was designated in the land grant and those who later held the mineral and water rights, between those who were hospitable to *extranjeros* and those who were strangers. It was clear on which side we would fall, but I still felt good that it was Flores or Morales and not McEachran or McIntosh. But for one incendiary flare-up in three centuries engendering a plaque, one might never sense the two lands that were Tierra Amarilla, TA.

The obstreperous nature of the 1968 Courthouse Occupation still shone in the quiet tolerance of the town, the swagger of the deputy sheriffs waiting for lattes, and in Ken's own rattle on authority.

"I don't let them forget it. They know I'll be baiting them any time they come in for a coffee. It doesn't stop them, and it doesn't stop me, either."

Well, it inspired me, the historical sign, the living memories, the living evidence, the art, and the attitude. I had to dip in my own oar with this fable:

How The Three Ravens Came to Be on the Roof of a Coffeehouse

The Old One in his bed rolled with dreams. Again, the acrid cry of ravens ruffled his sleep. "Damn crows." How could I have made creatures like that? Another blunt but twangy call, like a body sinking into a thin mattress on steel strap springs, scraped away the soft murmurs of sleep. Bolt upright, he swore. "I'll crush those black birds' bones, I will. The three of them."

Creation, like love, is a tricky business. The unwashed and unwanted always slip into the best-made bed, and so it had been since the old days when so few peopled the Earth. Strike a willow stick into life, it became a lethal snake. Coax a stone to swim, it grew teeth and a ravenous thirst for blood. Livened dust became ants with sting. And the once-made, cannot be unmade, even by The Old One. So he suffered his own progeny. So he had suffered these three ravens.

The raven He made with lava rock, oil and salt. The

rock brought color and durability. The oil made him sleek and evasive. The salt developed his attitude. What an attitude. He talked back. To his creator! It hadn't taken a day and it was Hey, big nose, does it have to be all road kill and? Nothing lively, fresh? It was funny. At first. Even at the height of the organized rebellion, He had kept his detached benevolence.

The Ring of Three, all ravens, was tired of the crumbs of scones, bits of panini, week-old road kill and the rest. So when He returned sweeping stars away from the moon, there they were—the three and every crow in the country perching in each window and doorway of The House, pecking at all who dared come close, chanting their croaking slogans:

Fresh beeves or no one leaves!
No more crumbs. Throw out the bums!
Creator's sneaky, be très cheeky.

If a god could sit down and cry, this would have been the time. What was there to do? Their numbers were too great. He stormed the door, and they flew up and roosted again on the window sill, or winged through the kitchen screen they had somehow propped open with a broom. No, a direct attack would not do. He must use his best weapon to clear the cawing rabble from The House, his own National Guard, the mites. Once let loose, all the ravens could do was turn around and around, seeking that incredible itch that could not be scratched. Some whirled until dizzy and fell down; others raised one claw, then the next, aiming and missing the only spot the mites attacked, the only spot that a bird cannot reach. Still others asked their mates for relief, but were met with the blackest stares. "I'm not puttin' my beak up there, comrade." Some cozied up to radiators, bedposts, chair corners, doing the raven fandango, all to little effect. The mites soon had the revolution in flight toward the river where in the shallows the birds found relief, drowned the mites and hopped all about, shaking their tail feathers like shy, abashed geishas.

Once He quelled the clamor and stilled his shaking sides, aching from laughter, a sad stillness fell over The House. He found the corpse of Uncle Marte, a quiescent favorite of His and cousin to that Damned Crow, in the kitchen doorway, flattened, torn and plucked by his fellows in their frenzy to escape the mites. From that sorry casualty, we learned that gods can cry. So can ravens.

Thus, even if He could have crushed his bones, He wouldn't. But something had to be done. After the occupation of The House had been cleared, the ravens turned guerrilla, dropping carrion on the sidewalk, sending crap missles at unshuttered windows, disturbing sound sleep with cackling conniptions. They were always in plain sight. Vigilant. Approached even slowly, they spread their mighty wings and launched into the sky. On retreat, they returned, cawing all the time. Finally, though no one knows how they did it, they entered into The Old Man's dreams in a litigious litany of complaint. That set The Old Man to thinking again, creatively.

One does not murder His creations. No, but change of state is not murder. And that's what The Old Man decided. It was mainly the voice he wanted to silence, always threatening to expose Him ("And to whom?" He wondered), always picking arcane bones with Him, always carping about humane treatment. But, too, He wanted to keep an eye on those birds. Even if they were quiet, they could cause no end of grief if they were allowed.

No, silence would not be enough. And jail would only be a bother. So . . .

In those times, by day, the Ring of Three had taken to perching on the veranda roof of the house next door in a constant conflab of crass comments and fracas-making bird-farting. When at a loss for words or out of gas, they set all in reverberation arrythmically pecking the tin roof. At night they disappeared, save in His dreams.

All that was to change with The Old Man's new idea. According to a passing coyote—no reliable person was near the place—who claimed to have seen the whole thing, this is what happened:

At dawn, just as I was slipping to my den, without warning, as is usual up here, a freezing rain pummeled the coffeehouse roof—and only that one roof—sticking those early birds instantly to the ridges of tin. Flap as they would, they could not get free. As I turned tail to run, I saw barreling down the road the fastest, blackest, biggest funnel cloud I had ever seen. It looked like the blacksmith's bellows, and it headed right for those ravens. Sure enough, it skipped up as lightly as a wren, hovered over them, whirling up feathers and caws, until all was quiet. Then it lifted and, like a coyote at dawn, disappeared.

And what do you suppose he saw then? Well exactly what you, yourself, can see to this day—metal birds, three steely ravens pecking at the tin roof—which is why, my dears, the place, when it was rescued from bulldozing demolition, came to be known as Three Ravens Coffee House, a place to find refuge and rest.

We had been forced from the road. The Vicissitudes had spilled our tourist cup. Now we were being lifted from the alfalfa strip, hoisted onto the flat bed of a new set of wheels. TA would recede into the dreamtime, but we would know everyone there and their history better than anyone in Santa Fe or along I-35. I venture to guess that we were better because of it, or am I merely justifying my spare stupidity?

Ten miles south of "Termaria," high up aboard the AAA flatbed's cab that was taking us to Santa Fe's tire center, we waited for the road construction flagger to wave us by the single lane. We lurched into gear following the lead car, when a flash of life from TA sparkled across our windshield. Wearing a bandana on his head, grinning broadly, and wildly waving a good-bye from the driver's seat aboard the road crew's steamroller was our host's son, Mateo Morales.

Take the Bus

THE BUS RIDE STARTED PLEASANTLY. The driver adjusted his cap and sunglasses and smiled at him as he climbed up.

"Can you let me know when we are just about at Mayflor?"

"Sure thing."

Buses were inviting. He liked this bus with its friendly driver. He had always liked being whisked away, riding high, able to look around. Buses were cheap, too. He jingled the change in his pocket and fingered the bills folded there. Alice would be pleased he was shopping for her. He wished Gamble's was still in business; he could just ask for something. They had known him. Frank would say,

"Hey, Lloyd, what can we do for you today?"

"I'm looking for a present."

"Lady?"

"Of course. What do you have?"

"Let me show you. I've got an idea."

Gamble's had never failed him. It was sad when Frank died and the store closed.

Now the familiar places where he used to buy most everything whizzed by the bus. These neighborhoods warmed him, sunny, homey and right-feeling.

The bus took the turn and moved uphill. Here the road was dappled in sun under huge trees hugging the road. Were they eucalyptus? He thought so, but he wasn't sure which kind. Hadn't they been brought here? For lumber? But it didn't work out. Something. The sunlight dampened under a passing cloud.

The bus rode on. The neighborhoods grew less familiar to him. Now the bigger, brassy, brash-feeling houses, set back from the road, stood, strangers in the trees. The windows looked back at him impersonally, blankly, like people on the sidewalk keeping their eyes fixed and distant. He shied away from the bus window, watched the other passengers. The lady with the crocheted shopping bag looked in a pocket mirror, tucking loose hair beneath her tam. Two high school students, one carrying a book, thumped their backpacks to the floor. He noticed the driver had changed. Had that happened at one of the stops? He hadn't seen that. Lost in thought. She was now a big, Latin woman who draped her uniform coat unevenly over the back of the driver's seat. She wore ear buds. She was chewing gum viciously.

He looked out again. Houses had disappeared now. He saw a few large storefronts behind parking lots, gas stations set around hummocks of lawn and red-leaved ornamentals, and something—was that a fire station?—fronting the street with three high garage doors. Just beyond, he saw huge blank-walled buildings through the maples and acacias, then, a round tower that marked the corner of one like a castle turret. The bus idled at a traffic light, moved under a lofty, goading arch spanning the road. He did not recognize this place. Did the driver call out Mayflor? No. That was worrisome.

The arch grew from twin geodesic-structured towers; in the center of the arch and supported by the gigantic, polished metal letters, M-a-y-f-l-o-r, a huge tulip in a filigreed circle spanned the road. The bus turned under the arch into a parking lot, stopped at a bus shelter that had a similar, smaller tulip over its own arching roof. He got off.

The mall had grown incredibly. It looked strange, foreboding and a bit frightening but, oh, yes, this is where he was going. To buy Alice a gift. She'd been so nice. He could afford to get her something. Something simple. The lady with the crocheted bag and the students got off. The bus left. He stood at the bus stop. Now, without the bus moving beneath him, he felt unsteady. Which way to go? What store was it? What store had it been? Where were those two giant eucalyptus marking the entry? He did not see the trees. Was it always Mayflor? He didn't remember.

He felt lost. He followed two women passing the bus stop. They seemed to know where they were going. One looked an awful lot like Alice. He walked a few paces behind, following them through the crosswalk, up a curving ramp bordered by polished aluminum railings toward high doors, under another Mayflor sign, over which hung another gigantic tulip circled with copper and brass leaves. When the women went into a lingerie store just inside the doors, one of them looked at him over her shoulder. It was not Alice. He walked past the shop, looking in the opposite direction, into the mall.

He saw a gift shop. Cards, figurines, baskets of soaps.

The man arranging a display of perfumes looked at him through goggle-like lenses. His eyes were huge.

"Let me know if you need help."

"Yes, I'm looking for a present."

"Well, we have plenty of them. Look around and let me know."

The clerk went back to his work. Lloyd looked listlessly at the shelves in the far corner. He didn't know. What would be nice? He wasn't sure. He worked his way toward the door, glanced at the man whose back was now turned, and slipped out of the store.

Down a wide passage lined with gaudy sports apparel shops and gewgaw stores, he passed a kiosk where a young lady shrugging a tattooed shoulder chatted with a bearded man. They seemed quite familiar. He heard murmuring. He looked away and up into the atrium soaring, one, two, three flights above him. The hall he had wandered down led him to this echoey vault that stretched up and off to the right and left as well. The unsteady feeling he had brought in from the bus stop surged. His legs felt tired. He was thirsty. He gaped at the skylights forty feet above. Clouds had gathered. The sun darkened.

"Can I help you?"

It was the young shrugging lady.

"I, I'd like some water."

He felt parched. A bit dizzy. He had been leaning on her counter.

"Well, there is the food court down that way."

"Food court?"

"You can get water at McDonald's."

"McDonald's?"

"Henry, maybe you'd better show him."

Henry sauntered round his side. He peered into Lloyd's face. "You're sweating, Bud," he said.

Then, Henry took his elbow. He noticed Henry wore a uniform jacket, like the lady had taken off and draped over her driver's seat. He didn't like the way Henry squeezed his arm.

"This way. I'll show you."

They moved off to the left, around other kiosks. He looked back but couldn't see the tattooed girl. Why didn't he ask Alice to come? He pulled to free his elbow but Henry tightened his hold.

"It's just down here. He indicated a narrow hallway. You'll see."

"What? Oh!"

He felt weak.

"McDonald's. The water. You want some water, don't you?"

"Oh, yes. And I'd like to sit down."

"No problemo, Bud."

He didn't like being called "Bud." He didn't like the way Henry steered his elbow.

"Here we are, McDonald's. Sit here, I'll get you a cup."

Henry steered him to a plastic seat and table behind the little white-picket fence that had an M worked into its stiles. The seat was harder than the bus seats. He wanted to be on the bus again going home. Alice would understand. But where was the bus stop? Now he was turned around. How many turns had he taken? Had he been there before? Maybe, but a long time ago. The mall was too big now. What had happened to Johnson Company? It seemed to him to have been just inside the door, but now that lingerie shop was there, those ladies, neither of whom were Alice. When had all that changed?

"Here's your water. Water with ice."

"Water."

"Listen, Bud, sit here, drink your water and I'll be back in a couple of minutes."

Henry put his hand on the table and leaned toward him, looking at him intently.

"Just stay here until I get back. Okay?"

He nodded but he didn't like the way Henry said "Okay." He didn't know who Henry was. He drank some of the water. It was cold. Then he wasn't thirsty anymore. He looked around. Henry was gone. The woman across the room tossed the end of a scarf over her shoulder. That's what he could look for. Alice would like a scarf.

He looked around for Henry. Out of the food court, down the long hallway, he turned right, away from the tattooed girl's kiosk. Three stores displayed scarves in their windows.

He looked at hundreds of scarves of knit cotton in stripes and snowflake patterns, of silk in paisley and dotted patterns—some had famous paintings screened on them; he recognized the painters—and of wool in dozens of shades and colors displayed in a linear rainbow of hues.

Later he was looking at blouses in more prints and colors, some sequined in spiral patterns on the sleeves. Hundreds of different blouses. For a short time he looked at bras and slips, but the sales clerks kept asking if he needed help.

Then he looked at kitchen gadgets. Alice would like this. It was for squeezing limes. Then tea pots with little yellow flowers on them. Table settings: plates, deep bowls, soup bowls, cups and saucers, salad plates, dessert plates, pitchers; in twelve different colors, butter dishes and salt and pepper shakers. Silverware. Hundreds. The chef knives sharp, sinister. He turned away.

Chairs! No, he couldn't buy furniture, It wasn't personal, and it wouldn't fit on the bus. But he sat in chairs, lay on beds all made up in a half dozen layers of sheets and covers and ruffles and bolsters, beds full of blankets, duvets, covers, coverlets, shams, pillows cases on puffy pillows, embroidered covers, shaggy comforters. He didn't know what kind of bed Alice had. He sat in over-stuffed, deep, leather reading chairs, on dining room chairs holding backs straight and severe, on floppy director's chairs and tall maple stools. No, furniture wouldn't work.

Then he looked for records. She liked music, but he could not find records—just these little things.

Ten stores sold T-shirts, dozens of T-shirts.

More showed shoes in the windows. What was her size?

More scarves. Music boxes. He liked the music boxes. Did she?

Glassware. Champagne glasses?

Mirrors, brushes, combs, make-up, a thousand little bottles, tubes, jars, vials.

In a bright store phones, computers, little things he had never seen before. Alice would not like them.

More shoes.

Ah, a store selling stationery. But the array, the incredible, confusing, overwhelming numbers of papers with matching envelopes and pens displayed in fan-shaped boxes and placards confounded him, put him off entirely.

He found many things Alice would like. None of them seemed just right. All of it whispered to him: buy me, buy me, no, me, me! There were too many things. Rows and racks and rails of things. Rows of racks and rails. Rows of rows. All sitting out there; you could touch each one. Not one floor, not two floors, or three, but floors and floors of things. He touched each one. He moved through displays and stores as in dreams, endless, nebulous seeking, never able to find. Finally he had wandered near the top.

He looked up through the skylight just overhead now. He heard the drops tapping on the panes. It was raining. The sky was black and wet. He was hungry. The weather looked cold, forbidding. Now, it poured. He didn't know where the bus stop was. In all the clutter, he hadn't found anything for Alice. There was nothing just for her here. He grew unsteady. It all seemed false. Thirst thrust its fingers near again. His throat ached dryly. Rain fell. It grew darker above him.

"There you are, Bud. I thought you were going to sit tight."

"Is this the guy?" Another man in the same bus-driver-uniform looked down on him over the driver's side of the electric golf cart Henry drove.

"I'm, I need to get something."

"Yeah, I know. It's been two hours since I told you to stay put."

"Alice. I need to get something for Alice."

"Listen, Bud, what is it you want, for Alice?"

"I want, I want to get something, something she likes. She is so kind."

"Sure, Bud, but we can't have you wandering around here getting lost, you've . . . . led us on a big chase here and . . . ."

Above the skylights, lightning crackled. He fell to his knees. The floor was hard and hurt. He felt very weak. The rain murmured above, he heard voices mixing with the rain. The bus. Alice. Why couldn't he find something for Alice?

"Up we go. Cal, grab his other arm there."

Cal squeezed hard. Henry dragged him up.

"We're going to help you here, Bud. Just sit up in the cart and everything will be all right. Can you call Alice?

That's right, sit there with Cal."

The seats were more comfortable. First the elevator, padded walls quieting the ride. He felt steadier then, better. The polished floors moved under him like a smooth river. He saw McDonald's; his cup of water was still on the table. He liked being whisked away from the confusion and lies. And Alice? Would she understand?

Timber

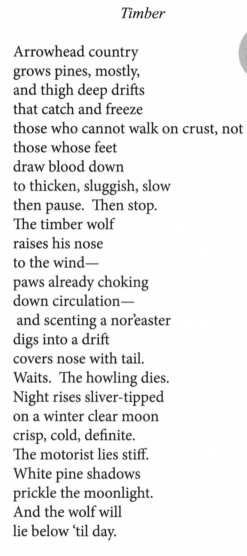

Arrowhead country
grows pines, mostly,
and thigh deep drifts
that catch and freeze
those who cannot walk on crust, not
those whose feet
draw blood down
to thicken, sluggish, slow
then pause. Then stop.
The timber wolf
raises his nose
to the wind—
paws already choking
down circulation—
 and scenting a nor'easter
digs into a drift
covers nose with tail.
Waits. The howling dies.
Night rises sliver-tipped
on a winter clear moon
crisp, cold, definite.
The motorist lies stiff.
White pine shadows
prickle the moonlight.
And the wolf will
lie below 'til day.

Chasing the Moon

I'D BEEN RUNNING AROUND for months, which in time turned out to be years, testing out Paul Bowles'[1] maxims on life, specifically, how many times I am going to see the full moon rise in this world, perhaps before going to the moon itself, or another place, or none, as Bowles would probably have it.

This fit of moon chasing rose slowly in me since having viewed his *The Sheltering Sky,* years ago already. Viewing the movie engendered another search, this for the book, used of course, of the same name, which seeking lasted, I think, two years. I used the quotation in my English classroom discussions. It caps the final minute of Kit's wondering, wandering film-life as she meets on screen the eyes of the then aged, now deceased author himself. Bowles utters mystically, telepathically, with no lip movement, the now famous, to my mind, prophetic words of conclusion[2] all of which—the full journey of mind, not the utterance—spun round my life and thoughts like the moon sweeping round the earth

1 Paul Bowles, expatriate writer, composer and traveler who lived 52 years in Tangier, Morocco. From his most famous novel *The Sheltering Sky*, filmed by Bertolucci, comes this existential musing:

2 *Because we don't know when we will die, we get to think of life as an inexhaustible well, yet everything happens only a certain number of times, and a very small number, really. How many more times will you remember a certain afternoon of your childhood, some afternoon that's so deeply a part of your being that you can't even conceive of your life without it? Perhaps four or five times more, perhaps not even that. How many more times will you watch the full moon rise? Perhaps twenty. And yet it all seems limitless.*

(sixty-five times in this span) for over five years before I began checking the newspaper for phases and times, before I began planning to be places that would afford a good easterly view, before I really began to peek over the horizon of meaning and understanding—a profound drop from my world to his, Bowles'.

The mania had lasted five years. At that point.

And without promising the moon now and delivering a cheesy pap by the end, just let me observe that for an itinerant scholar who has dabbled less in the exotic than the esoteric, who would just as soon pick up a hammer and saw as pen and paper on a Sunday, for one who moves through musical instruments like a musician moves through score sheets, though always playing the bass line, for me who under scientific scrutiny or, just as effective, by a quick observation of a casual reader of popular magazines would instantly be pegged as dyslectic-hyperactive-attention-deficient, for the whirling dervish I was to stick to an idea for so long (the rest of the mania is easily explainable—see above diagnosis) compares well with the accomplishment kindergarten kids on recess make building, launching, and recovering Apollo 9. That is, next to impossible.

The continuity that has built—the staying power, maybe of the moon but probably of Bowles' haunting melodic idea—tells me I am on the track of something important. Though Kit, the ill-fated heroine of Bowles' book, if one can be simultaneously existentialist and ill fated, thought the same thing.

ONE. Of course, the earth does not know the turning of the centuries or the anguish of Y2K (is that what we called it?), but the hoopla of our supposed movement into the twenty-first century—along with the arguments over which January first was truly the beginning of the new millennium (and I cannot now with conviction tell which side won much less which side was right)—all this balderdash at that time moved me from my armchair to a venue very close to that I write of now, a place dark, lined with redwoods and redwood shadows, hilly and exposing a magnificent vista of the huge wooded valleys twenty miles broad and, to the eye, forty sleek, north to south long, which separate the coastal range by the bay from Mount Diablo: the visual nexus of the lunar rise.

It was the last full moon of the thousand years which had witnessed the melding of Anglo-Saxon and Old French to the American prose that you now read; the raising of the Aztec temples, their bloody consecrations and their destruction under the hammer of Cortez y Isabella (*por mas glorificciones del Dio*); and the spawning of the thousands of names which to us define art, politics, philosophy and, in deference to the bellicose among us, war and mayhem. Of course, those of the previous millennia are with us still, St. Augustine for one, perhaps fewer but of broader penetration at the base of the collective human skull. This moonrise was to be our last with Chaucer, Tammerlane, Rembrandt, and Frank Lloyd Wright.

Into the last fresh air of my era I sallied warmly dressed, a flashlight secure in my fleece pocket, and in good boots made my way carefully under somber Monterey pines stepping over their raised root systems to my chosen vantage point. I arrived not long before what was for that isolated spot a goodly crowd populated, as is always true on momentous occasions like the last full moon of the millennium, by children in tow of fathers who are convinced that this is something for which it is worth waiting. And it was. It was worth the wait. Through the frond-like fog strainers of coastal redwood limbs from thin crowns sweeping down in graceful arcs like Gothic arches reversed, over the backdrop of the lone mountains' mountain, Diablo, Luna rose golden, clear and solitary for the last time over Dante's Hell and Paradise, too, an icon to the rise and fall of empires and ideas revealing our smallness in the enormity of the sky and in the bigness of our own imagination which, when healthy, is more a whole sphere than a dome. Of our little knot of fifteen, I alone, shared the eight minutes in a silence punctuated only by toddler questions answered by parental inanity, but mostly we shared a quiet profound enough to allow the sound of turning terra firma to echo from the slow-to-be-revealed moon and back again.

In some sense that was the real beginning of my moon chase. I suppose the turning of the century would have been enough, or maybe a harvest or blue moon in less busy times, to get me out in time to see the rise, but it was the giant, licked finger of Time, catching the page corner to start its lifting turn as if to throw me, clinging to the edge of that 2000th (or 1999th) page, onto the hillside at the close of what seemed to us all like a thousand years, to witness what Paul Bowles says we see but a dozen or so times. I wasn't out to prove him wrong; I simply wanted to see.

In the two years since the turn of the century, I have really seen the full moon rise but twice. If Luna were a softball, I would earn a batting average to put me in the minor-minor leagues as a moon chaser, two for twenty-six. My immediate reaction to Bowles' quotation which you see again following, was that I had seen the full moon already more than Bowles thought likely—I have always preferred walking at night, as it is good for thinking and more solitary—but paying close attention to his words, I had to admit that seeing the full moon, or nearly full moon, did not count as seeing the full moon rise. To arrange one's day or evening around the movement of the moon, it turns out, is much more difficult than might be imagined and, as you will see in what follows, those who run their lives by the clock and mostly live indoors even in the hospitable California climate, must plan ahead and move methodically to witness the lunar reveal as it happens. This is no well-advertised eclipse. In some sense it resembles a daily occurrence but, remember, only the moon at its full and coming first into view qualifies in Bowles' simple phrasing. Here are Paul Bowles' words coming from, in the book, the existential mind and in-amorous mouth of Port, husband of Kit, played in film, you must know, by John Malkovich, but words in the film coming from the forehead of Paul Bowles himself watching Kit enter, survey the Omar bar for something to connect with and not truly wanting whatever that something might be, leaving again. The words, spoken telepathically, in Bowles' own voice:

> Because we don't know when we will die, we get to think of life as an inexhaustible well, yet everything happens only a certain number of times, and a very small number, really. How many more times will you remember a certain afternoon of your childhood, some afternoon that's so deeply a part of your being that you can't even conceive of your life without it? Perhaps four or five times more, perhaps not even that. How many more times will you watch the full moon rise? Perhaps twenty. And yet it all seems limitless.

> Paul Bowles, *The Sheltering Sky (1949)*

Now this is not a literary exegesis or even a literary discussion, but the connection between the childhood memory and watching the full moon rise any number of times is a tight one, it must be admitted, though I resolved to deal first with the moon and later with that single afternoon. Somehow the moon seemed more accessible.

TWO. My first successful attempt to view the full moonrise, after the millennium's turn, produced a poem but little else in the way of insight; perhaps the intensity of the experience was distilled into the verse.

In some ways it was too easy. I checked the newspaper, which in many ways still acted as an almanac, publishing the phases and the moon's rise-times on a daily account of happenings in the sky, proof, I suppose, that even in the middle of labyrinthine, vast urbanites, the celestial movements are of at least moderate importance, more to Tomales Bay fishermen stubbornly trawling after the catch, I suppose, since iced salmon must come from somewhere, than to one riding the subway to his bank job. The newspaper, though, made it easy to get the information. If it had not been published daily, I wonder how long a time it would have taken me to log even two sightings. All I need do was show up at a place I could view and, since my swim club occupied a wonderful promontory overlooking the same Diablo Valley I had visited in 2000, it was most convenient to go there, set up a comfy lawn chair and wait, not a rugged wait, surely.

Nor was it, once again, a solitary experience. What amazed me, truly, were the number of distractions: skinny girls plunging in the pool, chatter of toddlers—always present, it seems, for these events; intermittent announcements of orders now ready, hot from the club's grill; fathers explaining the consequences of vivacious behaviors—running, ramming, rambunctious roiling; all punctuating a growing, expectant stillness and an infectious, atmospheric clarity undersung by rising choirs of crickets. And as if prelude to the moonish vaunting I had come to witness, a lone yogi, slim, smoothly feminine, who occupied the arrowhead of the promontory ahead of my arrival, greeted Luna's own arrival with heavenly contortions impossible to accomplish in the lightest gravitational field, stretching limbs toward the moonrise in supplication and praise to the woman who rides the sky.

Despite these earthly distractions, and despite my own internal distractions and lovesickness documented in the following poem, the celestial show vacantly occupied the proscenium of my attention. The diva lingered a moment in the wings, her sequins but lightly twinkling stage left, telling of her arrival. I waited.

Behind the line of treeless, now purplish foothills that moved serpentine to the south, which I knew in September daylight shone California-golden-brown, dotted and crested with broken, deep gray lava rock, my full moon dressed in white nickel cooled the moisture now sifting down from the chilling air, jealously straining all golden remnants of the sun in her concentrating seine. I focused and breathed the crisp air, shallowly, guardedly. The golden-purple scrim swelled, settled and silvered deeply as from behind a molten iron vein that had cooled, corroded, and cracked over eons as Luna's face had grown pocked. The innocent and great goddess of this night humbled all watchers by sheer platinum luminosity, quieted toddlers, stilled in a stretch the yogi, smoothed the swimming pool, and kindly stopped my heart a while. Her rise that shifts seas in bed magnetized us, positrons pointing east, calmed our urbane fearfulness, leaving only the taste of splendor on our gaping lips. Splendid it was, a regal rise. Heart-rendingly clear, richly argent, grandly detached, and intensely inhuman, Luna sprang free of the horizon. The crickets swelled suddenly and an errant father, perhaps for his second try, explained the physics once again to his college-bound two year old. The city resumed its atmospheric warming. The skinny bikinis returned to the diving board. I wrote this poem:

At full
rising behind ancient lava flows
now exposed on a distant hilltop
the moon appeared in silvery health.

I came resolved to meet her
just to see what would happen.

The fragrant, dewy lawn,
the crickets stem-wise clinging somewhere
down the hill singing their enjoyment
to each other
and the yoga-ist stretching at the promontory
were surprises the moon could know
nothing of but seemed to accept them as part
of her shimmering beatitude.

Family picnics and hot-tub denizens
strangely stirred just as ancient argent-head
revealed herself. Three teens dutifully
moved to our precipice, stood all of two seconds,

returned to the pool, their lives.
A new father explained, years too soon,
the movements of the moon and earth,
leaving out precession and its implications.

Alone at last with the risen moon
I became sensible of your movement,
turning your now silvered body,
opening vales and arching hills
skyward to her cooled touch. You
glory in the revealing, spread nude
before her singular gaze, giving her
an entrance, then, once on stage
stealing the show.

I can't usually feel Earth move
but, now, under moonlight, I feel
us both turning to her and strangely
sense the distance she keeps
and the invisible bond you two
embrace. I know years beyond the gaze
of human eyes, Earth and Moon
will lock—the Earth is slowing down—
too, that lovers, perhaps winged, many-eyed,
perhaps scaled, will have to travel, maybe
to this one spot, to some one spot
to view the moon and kiss, if that they do.
They will not feel,
as I have, the earth move.

Moonlight, thin in condensing air
streams now above me, my bald spot
illumining, shining back. Barefoot,

sweeping dew, sighing just softly
I myself move along without once
peering over my shoulder.

That would be bad luck.

It is easy to make too much of an event like this and, perhaps I have already, but though it is simply yet another notch in the walking-stick handle of moon chasing, the September 2002 full moonrise radiated enough awe through me to form the resolve I needed to prolong my chase. If nothing had happened out there, would I have gone back for more? As if behind those hills the something I had sensed now connected me more closely to the moonrise, to Paul Bowles' Sahara, to Kit's comings and goings, to the short breath of my own life, I resolved to return but to ferret out a quieter, more private venue. I wanted to be alone with the moon's rise.

THREE. How long had I known that two points define a line, a ray? Longer than I had known of Bowles. My moon-chasing ray pointed north from my post at year 2000, then two miles to the club promontory and, now, another three to a high point on the East Bay range, Round Top, at 1763 feet above the sea. At first buried under Orinda sediment, then uplifted to a tilt and exposed through erosion, it is a volcano, at night as quiet as death, formed, they say, ten million years back. The moon was faster in those days.

I was already far enough above the bay to the west and the Moraga-Orinda valley to the east, maybe 1400 feet, that I walked past Round Top to my promontory. The

Wicca in the neighborhood had years ago planted several of their stone spirals in the flats between the steep spines of hills I walked, as a fitting tribute, at least, to moon-watches if not as vortices attracting silver light. They were too deeply sequestered below me and the hilltops to admit moon-rising light; sensing their supernatural pandering, I stayed on the crests above.

I could see the bay, a quarter-mile below, ten miles out, and the Pacific, another ten miles further to the west, a view filtered by Monterey pine boughs, now darkly silhouetted and flattened against the brilliant, ruddy gold of sundown. The descending sun beckoned the appearance of my moon, and in the gloaming I turned my gaze to the east.

Know that sunset in coastal California is occasioned by a precipitous drop in temperature inland—in daylight, warm but late afternoons in summer, bring a jacket. What little moisture the air holds, too, changes its garb. Dew condenses to vapor and descends, fills the steep valleys until they spill over blankets of cloud, covering in turn more blankets of cloud. As startling and sudden as a moonrise itself, in the east, as far as I could see, perhaps as much as thirty-five miles, a fog bank had risen, it seemed, from earth or nowhere, stretching out to what now looked like a cloud-crowded horizon. Urgency took hold. November already, rains would likely obscure any winter excursions, so this was it; I willed the moon to rise and to rise quickly. It did not.

First, I am not a scientist. I am only sure the moon rises in the east, exactly where at any given date, I am less certain. The twists and turns of the coastal ranges disorient the natural compass within. I had to scan the horizon, itself as ill-defined as my sense of direction in its blanket of foggy dew; I looked for a silver glow above the clouds but saw none. Apparently, the quilting of fog suppressed any light from the moon that could guide me to the exact location of its rise. I say apparently, since something tells me it could have been the Wicca chants or long ago uttered spells that enveloped the spot and bound the light below. I was already getting superstitious. Where enchantment had lifted me high two months back, an eerie weirdness now pervaded my senses, much like the silently audible voice of Paul Bowles had sent the film version of Kit away from British society, itinerant, back to the desert. I peered now into a dark gray nebulosity for any sign of the moon. All I saw was a shape of amber light—something like the afterburn caused by sun watching—fitting to this place and occasion, saucer-like and silent, moving inexorably and directly toward me. If I could be transfixed by those spirals below, the fog out east, or the beam of amber light, solely or in combination, I certainly had no business out here alone. Moons be dashed. I wished for a comfy chair at home. Still, I could not wrest my gaze from the light which, thankfully or not, had apparently begun to slow and diminish in size. Finally, my flying saucer friend left altogether. I stood in darkness. A chill trembled me. The temperature dropped another degree or two, and dew fell. The cloud all at once liquefied, disappeared, and fell to the valley's floor, and there, already five degrees above the horizon that just moments ago fog covered entirely, stood the risen moon, a glorious *Luna plata*.

I had missed my mark while chasing rainbows—just as Paul Bowles, Port and Kit herself knew from their lives, actual and in fiction—also known as windmills, aka UFO's.

Walking back past Round Top I considered that

wanting to watch the moon rise only intensified the difficulty of doing so. I entertained the notion that Bowles could have envisioned any regular but unpredictable natural occurrence, such as the first snowflake to fall in winter, the initial lightning strike of a storm, or the lead school of salmon coming up stream. None seemed as easy or natural to a civilized man as watching the moonrise— after all, snow does not fall in the Amazon, nor salmon run the streams of the Indus. Though I had already proven both the charm and the difficulty of chasing the moon, against my nature, I was about to build a body of statistical truth to prove just how difficult the enterprise can be. Did Bowles know this? Well, am I an idiot?

FOUR. I was on time but was walking an arroyo toward my view spot. Missed it.

FIVE. I did not plan on rain.

SIX. Overcast.

SEVEN. Forgot.

EIGHT. Accepted a film invitation instead.

NINE. I had given up.

TEN. I had given up, but I did not die. The moon kept rising, goading the chaser in me even though I ignored the tidal pull; somewhere blanketed in that fog of three years before, I harbored an idea. If planning could not make it work, seizing a chance just might produce results. I became an opportunist. I moved toward the existential.

In Carson City nearly ten years after I watched film-version-Port shiver to his death in fever, eight since I'd read about the same event, and six since I first intentionally viewed the full rise, I charted my third entire full moonrise. I was not alone. It was romantic.

Carol and I pulled chairs from our room to the motel deck that overlooked a wide expanse of desert to the east. Conditions were superb: warm summer weather, an absolutely cloudless sky, enough desert dust blown up on the horizon to paint the moon ruddy. It was romantic, but then I said that already.

And Bowles had already said something that pulled on me beneath all my moon chasing, a grail—something rooted more in earth than sky—something some seek in the darkness of dreams—something best thought of but a small number of times, but remembered—something that explains, for better or worse, the insanity, inanity, and humanity of our chasing:

> How many more times will you remember a certain afternoon of your childhood, some afternoon that's so deeply a part of your being that you can't even conceive of your life without it? Perhaps four or five times more, perhaps not even that.

What would such an afternoon look like?

It looked sad from outside. Army blankets, touched by moths, dragged down from the attic, stretched over tent poles of straight-backed dining room chairs, a few legs of which showed worn wooden ankles and feet. The improvised tent hunched alone amidst broad lawn alight in green fire under the early afternoon sun. This was far from a Wild Bill tent or a small town P. T. Barnum one-night wonder. No, the warm wool wigwam was child's play, hopeful, experimental, innocent, and intimate.

Inside amid her chatter mixed with tiny golden rays that pierced the weave of wool and stung the air through moth-eaten holes, enchantment breathed its warmth around him, filling air he took in with envoys of the wool walls and pulses of her charm. She explained the rules of their game, a play of coffee club she had seen her mother give, in talk open and honest, gentle and encouraging, glowing full of love: ". . . and this will be our table. Today, we are having cakes and fruit with our coffee."

She indicated the graham crackers and orange slices she had found in the kitchen. The battered tin pot held lemonade a touch too sweet. Indicating to him the lone Naugahyde-covered kitchen stool, she prattled on.

"I always serve on my finest china here on the sideboard. Would you like a cup and a cake?"

He would.

"Cream with the coffee? Sugar?"

No, it was fine.

The sun wrought bars of light though the spindles of the straight-backed chairs patterning, striping and checking their faces and arms. The wool breathed the moist and soft radiance of innocence protected and simply being.

The stillness she fostered inside him and that she breathed within the tent imprinted on him sweet feminal charm, deep and abiding, waiting in utmost patience, privacy, and shyness while she centered the cup on his saucer, sealing remembrance with a kiss on his cheek.

Then full sun pierced the fly of the improvised tent, and seared the spirits of these youth with the feeling and tone of early summer: blossoming profusion without will, a shameless, exuberant twittering without sound just at dawn, and the upward push of grass that stains both knees and the ingenuous spirit. That shy enjoyment, a trust warm and palpable as sun, that cradling of intimate privacy, that ephemera of gender suddenly realized grew deeply into the full of their being. Their lives became inconceivable without these, forever afterward.

If I were that tiny boy, that half-hour under blankets would explain a great deal of me, much more than moon-mania does. And so Bowles was right, I found, and he was wrong as well. I had thought of that summer afternoon often, especially when shyness outweighed the salacious, when public gain threatened to over-tip private good, and when, as it has been much of my life, the company of the feminine—whether in male or female—beckoned. And since all that moon chasing and Bowles-prodding opened the flaps of that army-blanket tent again, I have thought of it more.

Did Bowles, in the persona of the careless, careening character of Port, warn us of the danger of inattention to these seminal events, a fig for their embarrassing simplicity? That seems un-existential. No, if it was a warning, it came only from the discouraged Port and should be discounted. Bowles for all he did in his artful life could not be so pessimistic.

For all that, I will go along with the occurrences and with the judgment of the experience. My running around, chasing the moon for a decade, brought me to my self, to my senses, to my childhood and back again. For if there is so much in so little a thing as I saw, raising the eyes occasionally to the heavens, or so long lasting a spark from inside a lumpy little chair 'n blanket tent standing in the back yard, then there is meaning in chasing the moon whether one catches it or no.

The questions I wish answered are really these: Do these events exist at all? In us all? Are we marked indelibly so early? Bowles, this time truthfully, accurately through Port, tells us: Yes, yes and yes. If so, then, as I ask my students, what? So what?

All my chasing after the moon made me aware not

just of the elusiveness of that heavenly body but also the transience of my own senses of time, of experience, of life itself passing. Would we express it simply, we would command, "Exist." But Bowles would bid us as he telegraphed Kit silently across the Oran café, "Yes, exist but exist mindful of whence you come and where you go."

Like the path of the moon, life moves on its own, changing ever so slightly a year, like the erosion of Round Top or the turning of millennia.

Hero

SOMETHING BIG HAPPENED last week among our hundred year-old row houses down by the river. It brought us out together.

A fire that started in an oil spill on her kitchen stove burned Señora Rosales' place to the ground. It was horrid, but that's not what I'll remember.

We streamed to the sidewalk across the street, watched some neighbors run in and out of their front doors, dragging out sticks of furniture or carrying boxes of photographs. Mr. Abalon lugged out a huge carpet roll, but once to his gate, he dropped the rug and grabbed his chest. There he stayed. Mrs. Johnson carried brass candlesticks and her granddaughter's painting of Jesus. She wept.

The fire now burst through the Rosales' roof. Distant sirens wailed, but the only help for poor Señora was from Lucky Luce spraying his garden hose around, more on his own roof than on hers. The fire felt hot on my face.

When *los bomberos* stopped at the tracks blocks away, Señora screamed. We tore our eyes from the fire. She slapped her hands to her cheeks, screamed again, "*Perrito! Dios mio!*" Her pug, Chachalaco, was in the house. "*Discúlpeme, Jesús,*" she cried.

Everyone knew Chacho. He was a little brown barrel on legs and barked like a fat man choking on chicken bones. He grunted like a piglet.

The tall kid who lived past Johnson's stepped up to her and leaned down to her ear. She clasped her hands at her chin, looked up at him, then closed her eyes, saying *"Por favor, mi hijo, por favor."*

He strode straight across the street. He lifted Lucky's hose, sprayed his Padres hat, doused his curly hair, and soaked his tee shirt and jeans. He handed Lucky the hose and strode right up that walk. I can still see his straight, bony shoulders moving under his tee as he marched to the Señora's front door.

No one spoke. People stopped running. They set down their loads and waited. Señora Rosales prayed. Flames roared and sirens wailed crescendo.

I was glad we lived in row houses. They were painted or peeling different colors but otherwise were exactly the same. Even in pitch dark, you couldn't get lost in any neighbor's house.

We stood open-mouthed—it seemed like fifty years—waiting. Now, everybody prayed. Then with a groan the kitchen roof buckled. Dining room windows exploded onto the sidewalk. We sucked air. Lucky wet his shoes with the hose.

At the moment fire engines rounded the corner, out comes the kid holding Chacho. He reached back, closed that front door, and walked right to La Señora. Everyone cheered. He held Chacho out to her. "He was hiding under the bed." The pug licked her face furiously, choking and grunting like mad. We all clapped like it had been some kind of performance or something.

That house is gone now, a front tooth knocked from a neighborhood smile. Even little kids still remember that fire. A few adults say it was foolishness to enter a burning house. Others say it was heroism.

The fire's not what I'll remember. It was great for the kid to brave death and carry Chacho out of a burning house though neither coming out nor going in is what I'll remember.

What I'll see forever are those squared, broad shoulders he carried toward the door. Entering the house, he was all the neighborhood's hope. Coming out, he was everybody's hero.

But what will always make me remember him is that when he came out, he closed the door.

Next Room

Washing his face
he could sense
the white wolf
in the bedroom.
She brushed
paper-thin walls
with her tail
and well-mannered
kept her feet off the window sill
but both eyes
on the parking-lot sky
below, looking for snow fall.

Steam smoked his mirror.
He shaved blind
rather than see
what stood behind.
When he looked,
razored by touch
soon enough,
only her white tipped
ears showed
behind the bed
listening at the window
for snow.

How he shut that door
he couldn't tell
but in twelve days
and twelve nights
he replaced his wardrobe
bedding
lamp
set up in the front room
washed and shaved
in the kitchen.
Swore he wouldn't go in there
until the howling stopped.

Signs

HE WAS A BLESSING. A miracle. It had been years since she had even thought about a man in a romantic way, much less come this close. Her pursuit of mathematics and spirituality of one sort or another seemed to be more daunting to men than her matronly shape, barbate upper lip, or the shocks of hair like winter wheat after a hard hail. Intelligence in a woman seemed more repugnant to the men she met than sweetness and light were attractive. At first she wondered whether it was the property and the retirement income that weighed in his decision, but like most fears she had about him the thoughts were dispelled when she learned to read his signs. No, she decided, he was genuine. After all, he had his own income, he had consolidated his property into bars of silver—an odd investment that somehow seemed to be wise—and he was kind, loving and dear.

She had learned to read his signs. A paced bustling through the night-lights or fullness of the moon simply meant the days were hot and meant for sleep. Moving slowly in the night through the soft blue tubes of glowing lights he'd laid bordering the drive, lights like river bends viewed aboard an overnight flight, meant another migraine. Deliberate walking through the property in the dusk or dawn—usually he pushed a wheelbarrow of gravel before him, a rake balanced akimbo atop the heap—meant he'd spent a full night at the height of excitement, and, often meant, too, the pinnacle of his desire.

In those dozen years, he had transformed her two acres just outside Hilo from jungle—dense, trenchant, infested, heavy and hot—to an airy, fluid, tropical wonder bounded by broad paths, pointed by flowering copses, shaded by palm and ancient acacia and sequestered by counterpointed ferns he called palapalai and his non-native hedges. From the windowless house—the sashes and frames he removed he'd safely stored in the tool shed standing behind the rhododendrons—she could see, even better at night, the passages he'd sculpted for the movement of air, around then up like ventricles, drawing the low-lying, earthy coolness through to the lungs of the house, pushing the heat from pools of sunshine up over the roof to rise above the columns of tree trunks. Breezes scudded along those paths. Swirling air busied around the copses and house corners. Into the open eyes of the windows, through the core of the house uncluttered, now, by walls and furniture and out the other screenless side, air wafted in drafts of coolness. It was as if he had visualized this, the night dew flowing in arteries and veins, freshly cleaned air in a clearing Hawaiian night, revealing the chill of stars. Through a decade she watched, as nightly he transformed the place from an air-conditioned bastion against torrid temperature and insidious insect to an inspired sweet breath of paradise. She too felt changed, transformed.

At first she did not recognize his doggedness. She raised much resistance when he suggested that like natives who build windowless, screenless, and sometimes doorless, houses, they too could let the mosquitoes fly in one side and fly right out the other. She doubted, loudly. But he wouldn't be doubted. His coaxing surged like his own migraines, relentless, but he also soothed like the night air, soft and cool. By that time it grew clear to her what he could do, and the nights of high excitement had convinced her to follow like the breeze flowing over the bedsteads that they had lately moved to the living room facing the entry. Understanding the signs, she would let the night air in.

One by one, in the still before dawn, he removed the screens, casements, trim, sills and jambs of each and every one of the twenty-six windows before he made any mention of the doors. Once she agreed, it took a month. And like his quiet ways in the morning, the breath of night-cooled tropical air soothed her, window by window, so when he finally told her he wanted to remove the doors as well, she was ready to assent. Out they went, all her doors and windows, to be stored in the garden shed in the rack he had built, more to assure her that they would be there if she wanted them again than to preserve them for some far-off need. Her barriers went down.

Those years before the stroke shimmered like mid-day heat. Intense, passionate, palpable. They were together always; discussed each action, each item, each idea before admitting it to the house. The excitement-bred desire grew as long as the full moon. They lived in each other's skin. Lived in each other's mind. Shed of the she and he, they were *they*. This seemed to her a fitting respite in a long life of career and struggle, an invitation to grow like the palapalai, to bloom like the acacia. In a harmony of color, she wrote her book: poetry, images, thoughts as clear and complex as the paths with which he circled the house and perimeter. It seemed to her that as his work expanded within a leafy shell, her work too, grew, filling more and more space like a lung ever expanding, inspiring, floating. She bloomed. Both did, she a morning glory vine, he a night-blooming jasmine.

And though she saw his daytime slumbers begin to lengthen, his nocturnal landscaping behind the screens of fern extend further and further away from the house toward the back of the property, her own days were so full of her work and punctuated by their frequent forays to re-supply in Hilo that his growing absence, his sometimes abandonment of her bed did not settle on her mind heavily. She took little heed of the signs.

Light as the shadow of a palm frond on the tea table, silently brushing across cups and cozy, she, lowering the book to her lap, wondered, "Had something changed?" A fly wobbled over the cut lemon. A puff of wind rilled her unparted hair. Vapors of the tea carelessly rose, dissipated. The palm shade revolved toward the patio corner. The teapot itself grew cold. What had happened? Her book slipped to the ground, pages turned in uncertain breaths of air. And like the spores and leaves that flitted across the table that afternoon, dusk thought to gather, to disperse, and then to condense in corners like a settling sigh. Was that the moment? She could not tell.

Inside, the quiet draw of the night had called him earlier than usual, and he found her in the dusk, still at tea.

Everything shifted. Now, she became his project. The stroke was mild; hardly a thing at all. All would return, he said. His kindness and care were matched by his skill and determination. Morning massage moved her blood. By his side at first amongst their palms, then along the road, step by step her trembling gait grew stronger, steadier, and, finally, unfettered. Their conversation was therapy.

Keep her talking. It moves the mind.

Companionship sprouted anew. Like the daily puffs that vented the heat, his ministering stirred her admiration and love. She was not alone. Now that she was his landscape for care, his own nights grew restful. Evening and early mornings, he tended to the yards. It was maintenance work. Though they talked of a cabana, he started nothing new. Like the gardens under his care, he saw to it first that she grew steadily stronger. She perceived his other projects looming ahead of her convalescence, so she talked of the other islands, a visit, an adventure. The cabana came first. She weakened at the prospect of resistance, read the signs, felt too well what that meant. She relented.

The new camellias had bloomed once when he started the cabana. There was little need for it, as the house was a large cabana, but it would improve the property and provide more workspace in rain. He began to work at night again, pouring the slab just past sunset, and tipping up walls in ten twilights, framing the roof in early dawns pure and clean, until the power was ready and he could blue-light the area. Then he could finish at night under both new and full moons.

She paced her work. The stroke dampened energy if not vitality, so in the house she shared with her sleeping lover where the mosquitoes moved along the drafts working their way inside, through, and outside again, she waited for the cabana to be done, for the nights to shorten once again, for the return of strength, for cultivation of their love. Each morning before the sun heated the back lot, she trundled along the shadiest paths to inspect his night's progress. She determined to make her move after the walls and finishing were done, before the planting season, before he could bring in the ferns and bushes which would shade and ventilate the cabana. She watched carefully; she knew the signs. She bought the tickets.

They wandered Kauai for five days, in the daylight. The nights wrapped them together under the blanket of the waxing moon that, on and on, grew full. He appeared, now in that moonlight, neither as laborer nor caretaker, but just as Ben. Himself again, untroubled by headaches, attentive, kind, loving, present. The atmosphere of another island invigorated him, did them both good.

Then, sudden as an afternoon squall off the Pacific, she could not breathe. She sweated.

"I have no pain, but I cannot catch my breath. I can't breathe," she told him.

"We're going to hospital. Now."

Later she told people that when you wake, you know as certain as life, that you have been opened like the lid on a tin of anchovies and have been welded shut again. She grew ever more colorful talking of it.

"It is like an ax blow followed by a shovel beating."

She enjoyed the theatrics as much as she enjoyed being alive.

"For women there is no pain. No feeling of congestion. It is just that you can't breathe. I thought I had pneumonia. And I felt so weak, like a composted angel fern."

Although it brought him inside again, the rehabilitation was harder. Just the surgery brutalized her body. Nothing functioned well. The weakness grew to weariness before it began to wane, but strength did not return.

Absence of exhaustion is not strength.

Like a wisp of acacia flower seen out of the corner of her eye, for the first time she glimpsed an end. Even in the stillness of her stroke, she had not feared, never thought of him leaving her. Now at her ending, she would abandon Ben to his nights. Alone she worried. She pictured him wandering the property in darkness, he and his migraines keeping company.

It really would not be that much different, would it?

I just won't be sitting inside while he sleeps or roams.

But she didn't die. She didn't recover. She progressed. And he assured her progress, attentive and encouraging and persistent as he had been before. Though, finally he returned to his feral ways as she gained her old habitude if not her strength. She hardly saw him.

Once again there were no signs. She'd grown strong and surprisingly quick enough by then. She came to him in the mud room where he lay stock still in the pre-dawn gloom of the guest quarter.

"I cannot move anything from my waist down."

He had been grooming gravels and sands along the blue-lighted ways. Stooping to examine a pod rocking in the wind over the walk, he heard a crack, felt, well, something. He took to his bed and woke an hour later, calling out. Heat pressed through the windowless, door-bereft openings.

Now there was nothing for her to read, no mugginess, no gathering thunderheads before the lightning. The stealth of illness, no, decrepitude, in the three years past unnerved her more than his condition: prostate cancer of the squamous cell type which had quick as a shark strike spread to the spine, causing fragility and breakage.

More than at any of the night-wandering times, she stood by. It was all she could do, all she could ever do in Ben's life, watch the signs. At times they were light, optimistic, but then, again hot, intense, dark.

The then current, well known routine of cancer treatment ensued. Surgery. Recovery. Radiation. Recovery. On and on. Its heat finally, gently blown away by a sunny disposition of optimism of the young physical therapist. Ben made progress. He would walk again. From the rehab facility, he hired a contractor to make the driveway more maneuverable, widened and smoothed for his return. With him home, she could manage. He had built manna in her heaven over that last few years. Time was for him to bask in the sun.

But like the sudden diseases that had been striking at the core of their world and their love, the fatuous insanity outside their paradise broke in the guise of practicality. To the bureaucratic mind it seemed a simple choice. If you can walk—the optimistic view—you do not need this wheelchair. If you need it later, it will be at your own cost, not a part of this occurrence!

She expected him to choose to walk—like beating back the jungle—she knew he could do it. But his family had arrived to retrieve him. Came in force. She permitted herself one epithet as they stormed the house to remove his books, clothing, effects, and bar by bar his silver hoard now grown in value by twenty-fold. She was sidelined.

She couldn't help herself as Ben's sister left with the last load. "Asshole," she yelled.

She had read *his* signs. But these were not Ben's. He was being ripped out of her life like a shallow-rooted palm in a cyclone, thrown across the road.

She didn't ask much, not even why, by what process, by what reasoning.

His elegant decisiveness had not left him.

"The feral cat will not be returning," he said.

He tried to smile.

"I'm tired now."

He turned his head to the side.

The afternoon inside the house had grown quiet and dark. The stifling heat moved beyond oppression in rank liquidity. High banks of cloud gathered and sat to the west, blocking the light but not the heat of the sun. The house, the cabana, the hollows of fronds and leaves of their paradise stilled each other in a pallid halt. The jungle beyond the property held its breath, waited as she did for a sign.

She lay her hands in her lap, still, one holding the other. She sensed only the movement of mosquitoes coming in the empty windows, one by one, taking a turn about the room then leaving on the other side. She thought of the mainland, of her daughter in San Francisco. She waited to read a sign she was unsure would appear. She watched the mosquitoes in, watched them out again.

Walkabout

THE TETONS DOMINATE. You cannot take your eyes from them. *Majesty* applied to anything else appears cheap. Approached from the north or south, they march along a craggy line, shouldering glaciers like sheaves of feathers, light; they soar, rocking and bouldering their way down to a treeline as densely green as the crests are searing white, mammoth gray. They shoot, catapulted monoliths, straight up from the moraine lakes they birthed, as if recoiling from the reflecting water's depths, flying in sheer lift from the plain over which they soar, a plain so towered over by majesty, it is named Jackson Hole.

The "hole" grew from the earth's overbite. One tectonic plate rose high, its neighbor to the east subsumed, creating a difference over twenty thousand feet from top to bottom of which five thousand has since been filled by glacial till and eroded rock. Still the Tetons grow as much as seven thousand feet in an awfully big hurry from the Snake River's bed to the tip, sitting on the shoulders of Mount Owen and Middle Teton, of Grand Teton itself. It isn't, perhaps, so special as far as mountains go—the eastern rise of the Sierra Nevada south of Lee Vining is certainly as sheer as escarpments come—but the breadth of the Snake River valley and the visual mass of crag-festooned Grand Teton make a spiritual difference.

The Tetons have sheltered eagle and hawk, bear and moose, elk and deer, cutthroat trout in moraines and gravelly rivers, beaver trying to slow things down, and, now, again, bison. The hawks elevate on the escarpment uplift to cruise the plain for rabbit, gopher, mice and yellow-bellied marmot babies; the eagles terrorize high-valley pica; moose tear reed bulbs from the slow end of mountain lakes and willow tidbits from along the flows in each deep valley that carry melt from glaciers and ice fields to the lakes below; deer startle in evening at lakeside as the beaver slaps a warning; elk herd together at dusk, and bison, ghosts rising like steam after a dewy dawn, surface to the plain from arroyos, their subterranean passages sodden with hoof-gashed pools. The solitary grizzlies climb high and far back from the single park road that trundles at a distance along the mountain wall.

This park road that the grizzlies eschew runs north along Cottonwood Creek from Moose Junction twelve miles to meet at Jackson Lake with US 89, the closest approach by automobile to the highest Tetons. Those traveling north to Yellowstone without intention to visit here, and local traffic from Jackson to the south and Dubois to the east avoid this slow road and travel US 89 five miles to the east. The majesty is certainly visible but not overwhelming from the faster road. Each year over one million drivers enter the National Park at Moose or Moran station to travel the road. Mostly they follow the advisory signs and warnings to drive forty miles per hour to avoid collision with elk, bear, moose, deer and bison; more often they drive thirty miles per hour or less looking for elk, bear, moose, deer, and bison, though few are seen roadside even during the dawn and dusk hours. Like the grizzlies, wildlife, especially that unbitten by the herd instinct, avoid the noisy and dangerous road.

That herd instinct becomes a behavioral issue

whenever an animal from the natural habitat does venture near the road. The bear jam—cousin to the traffic jam and log jam—clogs a road faster than a toll plaza on Interstate 80, giving rise to behavior nearly as fascinating to casual psychology as tectonic uplift is to geology. The behavior: backing into traffic, parking at obtuse angles in the roadway, shearing off doors left or suddenly swung ajar (sometimes all four of a sedan, though seldom are all summarily removed by passing vehicles), cantilevering out of car windows at various lengths and angles, running in heels, running in heels across the roadway without looking in either direction, running barefoot on gravel, running while photo-shooting, yelling, screaming, squealing, wildly gesticulating and iconically pointing, oftentimes at gray patches in bushes which sometimes reveal themselves as rocks and sometimes are nothing at all, but done in a colorful pantomime or cacophony of cast worthy of a high-end consignment store specializing at once in Hawaiian and military garb. This behavior is all quite natural, under the circumstances. After all it is, at least we think it is, a wild animal!

Quieter, less disruptive behavior is the more common and perhaps more unnatural: The Cadillac Escalade, "the most acclaimed luxury SUV ever," according to its maker, lumbers to a halt at Teton Glacier Turnout on the Park Road. Depending on the month, according to the Park Service, it carries 2.4 or 2.7 occupants—apparently it has a larger capacity in summer—but an observer cannot know this since the windows are heavily tinted, no doubt protecting the occupants, however many there are, from untoward ultra-violet radiation and from that uncomfortable feeling that someone, someone the driver does not want to encounter, is watching. The wagon idles at an eighth-gallon-per-minute clip for .0625 gallons worth, when the driver's side window lowers to half staff, allowing the Nikon Zoom telephoto lens to protrude just enough for the Nikkor 80mm-400mm drive to snap twelve shots of the Teton range in eleven a. m. sunshine. The cannon barrel is withdrawn. The tinted slab rises. All is as it had been for an added .125 gallon stint. Then, after lighting the highway at four points of flashing amber— or perhaps not, lurching, instead, heedless of indicators or passing autos, it owns the road, doesn't it? The most acclaimed luxury SUV ever roars its 2.7 occupants north to the Jenny Lake Visitor Center, another four miles and .4 gallons, up the road. The interlude has taken all of a minute and a half.

Now, given that the Park Service estimates the average visitor's stay at three hours per head, these visitors have communed with the glaciers of the Teton range for all of two point seven eight tenths of a percent of their visit, (0.00278%). That in itself is not unnatural. What may be, though, is the idea now lodged in the Escalade occupants' brains, "I have visited Grand Teton."

The average stay at Jenny Lake Visitor Center is not a published statistic, but let us follow a visiting family in the month of July, the most popular time to arrive, and see what might be a typical excursion through this area. Brett and Salindra, Marci, the eldest, and the boys drove two days from Valparaiso, Indiana, are on their way to Yellowstone, and half an hour ago entered at Moose station south of Jenny Lake. Brett had done his homework, so he heads directly for the Visitor Center, a mountain cabin, porch, rocking chairs and all, surrounded on three sides by tarmac. Salindra heads for the flush toilets the other side of the Center, another cabiny structure, slightly larger, but first puts Marci in charge of the boys who have already mounted the porch steps of the concessionaire's Jenny Lake Trading Post and are clamoring, one for ice cream, the other chips and Pepsi. Marci dutifully takes them inside.

Brett has already viewed the topo-model of the Tetons, scanned the geological exhibits, and is second in line to ask the Ranger where to buy the Jenny Lake boat tickets. He will be told—the fifteenth repetition of the morning—"Straight up that path (indicating the asphalt walkway flanked by split rail fence) to the dock." But he does not have to wait since the man in front of the line has the same question. Brett is out the door: time elapsed, two minutes, forty-two seconds.

He will wait, he knows, for Salindra, so he goes to the Trading Post, where Marci is perusing the Huckleberry Jam display. Corey gazes into the freezer; Morey fingers each bag of chips as if he were reading Braille, both working on a decision. Brett examines the camping gear, the Pendleton blankets and jackets, glancing once in a while at the door, which swings open four times a minute. Halfway through the revolving key-chain display, he sees his wife enter; she goes right to the stuffed animals, beaver, moose, bear, squeaking and squealing with Marci, "How cute is this!" Brett moves to the boys, jostling a choice from each, and, after a short wait in the cashier's line, buys the treats, getting a Blue Bunny Ice Cream Sandwich for himself, which once on the veranda of the store, Salindra makes him split with her. Marci disappears into the store to check the freezer. The family lounges on the benches consuming the ice cream, chips, and Pepsi, then strides to the dock. Total time at the Trading Post: forty-five minutes.

Now, the Beckers may be out of the ordinary, for they will take time for the boat ride, twelve minutes, the ascent to Inspiration Point, thirty minutes, viewing, three minutes, the descent, seven minutes and the return boat trip, twelve minutes more, plus waiting time, all told: about an hour. Most never make it off the tarmac.

Back to find the Dodge van among a hundred others like it parked just past the store and on for a peek at String Lake, Jenny Lake Lodge, Jackson Lake Dam, a rest stop at Lizard Creek before the drive to Yellowstone. This fills out the three hours the Park Service estimates for the average visit to Grand Teton National Park. For the five—statistically reduced to 2.7—at three hours each notwithstanding other minor adjustments the Brett Beckers will count for 8.1 hours of "recreational" visiting but in reality will have spent in aggregate, three hours and forty-five minutes at the store, 120 minutes boating, three hours five minutes hiking, fifteen minutes enjoying Inspiration Point and five family hours driving. Driving and time in the store win out.

Back up that tarmac to the boat dock, still more telling of the investment visitors make in nature, is the Ranger Station proper, one eighth the size of the tiny store, where one is likely to encounter the few visitors registering for backcountry stays. The station is not hard to overlook, nor should it be for the business it conducts: in 2010, 30,582 visitors applied for stays in the backcountry, requiring hiking at elevations in excess of eight thousand feet anywhere from fourteen to fifty miles, sleeping gear, shelter and some means of eating and/or cooking, a total backpack weight of thirty-five to fifty pounds. The number fell to 20,902 January through September, 2011. The falloff followed a like, overall decrease in visitors, but leaves the ratio of backcountry campers to those sleeping indoors, in lodges and in cabins, at eight to one, and in relation to all recreational visitors, one to 127.

Now these hearty souls are on the opposite end of the spectrum from our Escalade-clad visitors and the Beckers. They are visiting the Tetons. Encounter them at Climber's Ranch showers, just returned from a five-day hike along the Teton Crest Trail, Death Canyon, or Alaska Basin trail, scruffy, in most cases sodden, and hungry to the core.

They have been exposed to what the mountains offer, besides the view: thunderstorms, usually incorporating hail and sometimes snow, high-altitude solar radiation, ants, bears, poison ivy, icy waters, treacherously sudden winds, and fatigue. But they have also breathed the freshest air on the continent, seen stunning, rare, and close-up views of the god-mountains, jarred at close encounters with grizzlies, marveled in moose and elk sightings, touted and tolerated civil and uncivil comradeship, and, after an hour of preparation, satisfied hunger, gorging on gourmet, freeze-dried beef stew.

A five-day backcountry hike in comparison to the one-minute-wonder visit to Teton Glacier Turnout, outstrips the ratios already struck, 7,200 to 1, that is seventy-two hundred minutes to one of communing with Tetons. Even discounting sleeping time under the stars (resulting in 4,800 to 1), it is not hard to argue the value of one experience over the other. Of course, the carbon footprints cannot be compared justly. A less extreme comparison with the Beckers moves a step closer to experiencing Grand Teton, but a baby step.

Well, we can't have 2,669,374 recreational visitors, the number documented in 2010, tramping the same backcountry trails the moose and grizzlies do, not if we want moose and grizzlies. Nor would, nor could the visitors do that. Too, that huge number will not fit the respective quarter of a million campsites and lodge/cabin beds; we would have two million folk sleeping under trees.

The Park Service has done a job diversifying both places and activities that will still draw visitors into the park and into the wilderness: hiking on improved, annotated trails at levels of difficulty suited to the wide range of the ambulatory; kayaking and canoeing on both lake and river; boating, especially on the large Jackson Lake; biking on trails devoted to two wheels; viewing wildlife far off the road; climbing, including technical climbing; alpine hiking; backcountry sojourns; Ranger talks at campfires, points of interest, museums, visitor centers, and Ranger stations; lodging to suit those who need clean sheets, a solid roof overhead, or just a sleeping bag with or without tent; and information, plenty of it, about it all.

But note that miles and miles of paved road is not a feature of the park to be touted but to be used sparingly. The roads bring the two and a half million in each year, but, Americans! Get out of the car!

Yes! Go with the idea to extend the stay beyond the three-hour average, with the promise to leave the road, the car, the carbon behind. I offer an added model for doing so: a solitary traveler from the other side of the world.

His lean frame perhaps made him look taller. Too, the loose fitting clothes: the short-sleeved shirt dangling on his frame, cascading over empty-pocketed cargo shorts out of which skinny, browned legs fell into knit socks that drooped over leather street shoes. The shirt was a pumpkin-orange print faded over a yellow background.

"Is this the path to Bradley Lake?" He said.

"Yes, eventually."

He strode giraffe-like over to the signpost to read the map. We'd hit the trail while he read, but it wasn't long before his sauntering, long-legged gait overtook us. I stepped off, letting him pass. He wasn't in a hurry but just as rapid as the stream running behind us.

"Thanks."

"See you at the top," I said.

He said nothing else and soon lost himself, blending with the greens of the trees and meadows along the trail.

The Lupine Trail, not a particularly difficult one, starts along a gravel approach road two miles from the paved Park Road and winds through Lodgepole Pine forest along and over Cottonwood Creek, which drains Jenny Lake to the Snake River. Frequent breaks in the forest allow wildflowers of all shapes and colors to bloom prolifically and for the copses and stumps of pine to invite mosses and burrows into the forest. Some fallen timber show bear sign. The trail gently rises out of the staging area, then switches back on itself a half-dozen times, climbing fast before splitting at the junction of the Bradley and Surprise Lake trails. Both lakes are up another three hundred feet.

We rested and dozed at the junction and finally agreed with Carol's tired feet that going back down was the best use of our energy. It would make a pleasant, sunny hike, short though it was.

At the trailhead, here he comes again, his six-foot two frame swinging along the trail exactly as it had started.

"Did you get to Bradley?"

"Oh yes. 'ad a bit a' it up there, too."

I noticed he did not carry water. Indeed, he carried nothing at all but himself. He admitted to drinking from the stream.

"I suppose I shouldna 'ave."

Yes, I suppose he should not.

"Are you British?" I noticed his accent.

"Austral'n."

"Here long?"

"On a bit of a walkabout."

He had been traveling, and, presumably, walking-about for three months and wasn't quite finished yet, though he couldn't or wouldn't tell me where he was headed next. Before he climbed into his own Volkswagen van, at least ten years older than mine already approaching 30, I derived the idea that here was a man close to nature, in little need of an excuse to ramble around the American West, mostly on foot, diminished of the chains and protections of material goods, doing simply, directly, profusely what he had inherited from his own aboriginal countrymen, a sort of spirit-finding ambulation. The implication was not lost on me. He had not been on a hike, as the two of us had taken. He sought not for natural beauty itself, but for himself, sprung from natural beauty. It was not pictures—definitely not rearranged electrons in silicon—he wanted. His walkabout led a quest, opened a perspective-forming solution to his life's problems. He did not carry his world on his back—given that the van he bought would soon be sold again, I surmise he carefully took back with him what he found, returning with much more than he carried, but weighing much less.

He had to be from overseas. The distance and limitation-shorn regalia of a shirt, shorts, socks and shoes, a mat and shelf in the van, freed him from "pushing his barn down the road" at seven miles per gallon; still what majesty poured into him could be put in neither a pondside shack nor an entire fleet of Escalades. Would Americans take note?

The glory of the Tetons have to reflect a high value, higher than Nikons, Blue Bunnies, and Pepsis. *Inspiration* means to breathe in, not to stop short. Leave the shopping behind. That is something for a trip to the suburban mall. Invest the time to have an experience in and with the natural world. Surround yourself with that not made by man; leave the watch and the camera locked in the trunk. Put on rugged clothes and a rugged mind. Breathe deeply the mountain air (and drink lots of water). Welcome and be ready for the rain; the bears are. As a first step, get out of the car!

Take the trip to Grand Teton National Park. Before leaving, take a vow on the mountain itself to spend an hour, yes, out of the car, away from the road and buildings, out of sight of others, to commune with what you find there, to commune with what you bring there. This might feel odd, at first. It could be cold but won't be dangerous. Let the majesty work into the lungs, into the skin, easily, as slowly as it takes Cascade Creek to feed Jenny Lake her breakfast. Breathe in your majesty. Let it work.

Federal Case

He became the family hero
someone mantled with pride
someone we could emulate.
Finally, a lawyer doing good.

They say he saw an opportunity
somehow in the law library
to become the selfless
hero to the unheeding unheeded.

Preparation and patience
were his strong points
and a sort of fearless
common sense-
the kind that knows
what to do when a hunter
grins and turns
his rifle your way.

He did not find it hard
to build a case
for a defendant
on the loose.

An Elliot Ness
in reverse, the good Fed
defending the evil one.

Three years
and a week
on District Court
he stared down
deer lovers, farmers, and bounty hunters
for protection
of the Minnesota
timber wolf.

The win, so technically brilliant,
stirred Norway pine needles
near Lake Namakon
where a white wolf
scented an early fall.

Last Thanksgiving

HE CALLED IT THE WALK OF THE HUNDRED HELLOS. When he began fifteen years before, he initiated greeting each person he met on that three-mile morning walk. Two point eight miles short form, three point two following the shore. He greeted the hooded squat runner, busy, dedicated walkers waving their arms like grandfather clock pendulums, couples chatting ensemble, young mothers strolling babies, the dressed-for-success walkers on lunch, fitted with idiosyncratic white tennis shoes; trios, singles, homeless snoozers, indigents; those sporting earbuds, headphones, or wing-shaped ear transmitters; the Asian ladies, one always with a flower on her hat, and ancient walkers; the Turk with the carved cane, huge athletes, the happy-talking descendants of Louisiana shipbuilders; the shy, the sacrosanct, the ebullient, the young on fire with life; sashayers, joggers, long striders, and plodders alike. All these greeted his morning world. And once started, he could not find a reason to stop his greetings. It seemed cold to pass anyone in silence.

Even today, with a chicken ready for the oven and the cranberry dessert to assemble and bake, he carefully dressed for the November chill. His first hello came approaching the crosswalk, even before he had pulled on his gloves.

Odd. I've never counted how many. A hundred seems too large a number. He called out "hello" to the empty chamber of the pergola. For three years he had honored the little black man who had worn his multicolor coat year-round for twelve years by rough count, later growing thinner by the week, moving slower and finally gone. All gone but his own hello.

We shared a schedule. Always met right here.

Sometimes, others passing, thinking the greeting was for them, responded in kind. But the hello was for his ten-second companion of twelve years. A vocal memorial.

Who will take over now? " Good morning. Hello."

He passed the four birders, the tallest pointing to a bufflehead duck, just a speck on the gray lake. By now he knew all the ducks, mostly mallards and coots by the shore, and could predict by locale which they were.

He had slowed. The lake walk was longer, and he greeted more fellow strollers each year.

No need to wait. It can never be the walk of the two hundred hellos!

Perhaps he shouldn't have left the oven heating, the walk taking so long now, but he thought less of the energy wasted but the time saved. He would put the bird in as soon as he returned. It would take two long hours at the low setting. It was best roasted slowly after browning. He wanted to be sure. He wanted it to be beautiful and savory even though no one would eat it.

No, no one will even think to eat it. Not the others either.

He had risen in the still-dark early chill. He changed the sheets, replaced them taut-tucked and smoothed each layer as he laid it on. He fluffed the pillows.

The less mess, the better. Everything tidy.

In the kitchen, he crushed the rosemary with the pestle, adding olive oil and garlic as he ground it. He washed his hands, twice, under the warm faucet, sudsing hard, patting them dry. Touching the oil paste lightly, he slipped his slick fingers under the skin, separating it from the flesh, slowly, not tearing through, adding more paste as he proceeded, spreading it over the thighs, the breasts and what he could reach of the back and legs. The remainder of the paste he spread over the loosened skin, salting all, dashing pepper over the whole.

Let that sit covered now while he took his walk.

He had already bathed and shaved the night before.

He'd heard that hair and nails continue to grow. That was false. He thinks the flesh and skin shrink some. It can't be prevented.

He patted the chicken, covered now on the counter. It would fill the house with the aroma of rosemary and garlic.

Yes. A delicious aroma when Artie stops by at three.

Artie had been a good neighbor these years. He knew he could count on Artie. As he drew the door to, he looked back at the countertop array all ready: parsnips, carrots and the potatoes lined and grouped, the pears and greens for salad, the soon to be beautiful chicken, all in order. The oven was on. It was the right thing to do.

Even though he thought of the time, he took the shore route.

Just a little bit longer. That's all right.

The geese were plentiful around the boathouse.

Do they taste wild? No, these are city geese. They don't really come down from Canada, don't feed on northern roughage.

He thought of the wild game dinners Roger had thrown: geese, duck, partridge, venison, even bear at times. The aromas enchanted. The table full of all the best Roger's hunting brought, accompanying all with bowls of wild rice, garden potatoes and carrots. He had the game only at holidays, and only at Roger's. If Karen's dad came over—a rarity after that first time—the birds and beasts stayed in the freezer.

And so many at the table then. Ten or more. That was feasting.

"Good morning." It was the soul sisters. They smiled big.

"Happy Thanksgiving." They called out in unison.

"Likewise." Happy Thanksgiving to you all. To you all.

Yes. It was turkey on that first time. Julie was three. That shifted the balance. John and Marty had gone to college. Three to two now. That had justified their first hosting. We combined families too. Karen had his help with the fowl. She proved herself.

We had a crowd.

Turkey. Banal, but everyone had enjoyed the effect. Dishes clattered in the kitchen, the felicitous sound penetrated the living room, ushered by the wafting aroma of coffee. Still it didn't wake the snoring men there. Karen's pumpkin pie did that.

"Pie and sweet whipped cream," she announced.

It felt domestic. Since he had never hunted, did not care for the brash coldness of guns, it had been a farm-raised dinner. Their first, their every feast lacked the heady, wild flavors Roger plated. No matter. He loved to watch Karen fuss.

No one knew how to use spices then. Salt, salt, salt. The pepper made Dad sneeze. Huge sneezes. Thunderous sneezes.

The wind gusted, beating strong and loud around the

point. The city came into view, green glass sheets trimmed in silver steel. The graceful architecture caressed the lines of the shore, and the gulls swept arcs between roofs and water rills. It all fit. There was nothing sharp or out of harmony.

Flowers! I was hoping Lottie would be open this morning!

He entered the little shop.

"Good morning, Lottie. Thanks so much for opening for me today."

"You, my dear, are not alone."

"How much are your alstroemeria? I like the *aurea*. Bright and cheerful." He thought of the table set in white with the blaze of orange and red-orange flowers at its center.

They last a long time. Not necessary. But they will last.

He slipped the bills out of his back pocket. "Three bunches. Wrap them for a walk, would you?" He gently placed the floral cone in his backpack, zipping each side up a third.

All my Hellos will enjoy seeing these.

He felt lighter with the bunches sprouting from behind. It seemed that the joggers smiled more at this flowery "good morning." The holiday seemed to bring out the runner in everyone in town.

"Good morning." A big family.

"Good morning." The 'sweeper' at the Lake Club Restaurant. "You do such a clean job." He smiled it. He meant it.

"Good morning." An Arab woman brightened into glee. Her scarf fluttered.

He paused at the estuary outpost to look down the

lake to the pergola. The sun broke out a minute on the dome of the church. The wind died down.

He remembered a long-ago church dinner. Where had Mom been? He couldn't recollect, but she hadn't come.

Oh, his father blamed the spinout on the icy road. He thought they were on fire. Red glow in that snow bank.

"No," both brothers laughed even though uneasy, "It's the brake lights, stupid!" No one talked about why it happened. He recalled those lights. Red devils dancing on the snow.

No, Dad could not be trusted. It grew worse later. The year Janey was born—his mother was gone, this time hiding out in North Dakota, mulling things over—Karen wouldn't drive the twenty miles to "find a drunken oaf in a cold kitchen." His father had bought the turkey already, but he was slurring words every time they called him.

"You have to go up there to get the bird," Karen said. "He can eat with us. It will be better this way. I don't want to expose Julie and the baby to disaster."

He talked it over on the phone. His father smoldered, sullen.

"You're stealing my turkey."

Argument was senseless. He drove the twenty miles, took the turkey out of the refrigerator and told his father to come Thursday morning.

"You're stealing my turkey."

"You are invited. We'll do everything."

Yes, Dad. We did steal the turkey. I wish you had come.

"Oh, flowers." They were the Asian ladies, ancient, older than he, still lively.

"Good morning. They're alstroemeria."

"Cheerful. Pretty. Happy Thanksgiving."

He waved and crossed from the promenade to the shore trail. The canvasbacks were usually bobbing around on the cove there. Their iridescent heads played red and dark in the sunlight. Their small numbers, their rarity, made them welcome, though the mallards were every bit as gorgeous. He saw six in the cove. They seemed to be waiting, just floating along. Perhaps thinking of the south, of leaving the lake soon.

His circuit nearly done, he began to think of other things.

Keep your mind on the dinner. The table setting.

He had ironed the Bertozzi, yesterday. The flowers he bought would stand out well on its white field. The vase picked up the green hand-stamped filigree. The platters were set, salad bowl in place. Serving utensils still needed.

How many place settings?

A full table seemed presumptuous. They would think no one came, not that no one was invited. Artie would come for his last week's mail. Two would remind every one of Karen. This was not about Karen. He had done without her for years before the end. No, two settings would not do. One might be enigmatic enough, but he settled on setting none. Not one place setting.

That tells the story. Life is a no-host table to which no one is invited. We come. Unbidden. Not unwelcomed but never looked-for.

He baked the crostata first. He wanted the chicken still to be aromatic at three. He peeled the parsnips and carrots, careful to remove as little as possible beside the thin skins. He oiled them little. He pierced the potatoes. The yams were in the oven with dessert. They would take the longest. He positioned the pie server and the carousel on the cloth. Trimmed the flower stems and one by one placed them in the vase, standing back occasionally to see where the next should go. Finished, he centered the urn.

Too early for the pears.

He wiped the wooden salad bowl and clipped the stems of the spinach between his thumbnail and finger. A serving for three filled the bowl. He roasted the walnuts and set them to cool. The raspberries he added to the greens. The chicken took the place of the dessert in the oven. He reduced the setting. The yams were still a bit hard.

In the kitchen he worked quietly, methodically. He cleaned as he moved along. He would run the dishwasher when the table was finished. Everything would be clean.

The table was glorious. The alstroemeria at the center blazed through crystal. Around the middle of the white cloth he grouped the platters: the golden chicken, yams to intensify the flowers, nutty parsnips mingled with carrots, the greens highlighted by raspberries and the white of pear slices and the brown candied nuts, the gravy boat, clear succulent liquid, and the rosy-center crostata, still warm.

It is splendid. Seventy-seven Thanksgivings.

He uncorked the cabernet.

Let it breathe.

He washed his hands, inspected the kitchen carefully. Set the dishwasher.

It will be all right.

Later he tipped the wine bottle carefully to the glass rim. The wine spilled its deep red, fruity aroma around the stemmed bowl.

It is all right. It will relax me.

He tasted the wine, let the glow flush his cheeks. He corked the bottle. Sipped again. Deep down he felt the hot grip of want, the muffled screams of desire.

First glass in what? Thirty-two years? Just one glass.

But he brought the glass and bottle with him, setting them beside his reading lamp while he undressed and hung the clothes. He carefully folded the undergarments and socks. Put them in their drawers. He sipped twice more before slipping between the sheets.

Now the second glass. You won't have to finish.

He poured another. The wine filled the room, filled his senses. His body's warmth filled the bed. He let his breathing slow and become regular. The wine wound its way through him and swirled around his head pleasantly. He breathed. The heat rose within and without.

I'm certain. He opened and poured from the vial he'd placed under the pillows.

How much? I don't remember. He emptied the vial.

He circled the mixture in the glass. He breathed.

Does it matter?

He drank.

In the kitchen the *cavatapa*, his long hidden corkscrew, sat out on the counter, forgotten. At table the dinner waited. Artie would come in an hour.

A single orange-spotted petal fell to the white cloth.

Trolling

I'VE ENJOYED GOOD LUCK over the years even as my eyesight darkened, because the lake bottom that drops off where I trolled for walleye bellied in close to shore, very near her dock anchored on posts just yards from the draft of deep and dark water.

I imagined the fish's-eye view, underwater, the lunkers waiting, below in the deepest water, for minnows and small fry to venture too far out from the safety of shallows. I'd visualize them, the big fish, lunging upwards, lashing out with open jaws to scoop three minnows at a time into their maws. In those silvery flashes the big fish would first see my boat bottom and then the underside of her dock suspended above their element, doubled in reflection, on the surface and seen above it, too, spreading out from shore in the direction of their deep haunts. Over those precincts I drifted, delving for the big ones and for something else.

Quite young I had learned to canoe on a line, even in wind, by myself. In my family I'd earned the name "he paddles north." Riley, a girl still, dangled tanned legs into the lake at the end of the dock, crisply cutting the ripples she'd made with her feet, but never listlessly. At the same time she groomed her ever-present spaniel with her small, bare hands. The dog lay, paws at the very edge of the white-painted boards, snoot poised over the water as if to lunge at a passing perch or sunfish.

This was the way I knew her through childhood and

our school years, and after her marriage to Tib: out there for years with her kids, counting down from three to one, then much later alone again, except, with maybe four successive spaniels over time, always with the dog, the same breed. Then the wolves came.

I had known Riley Parsons before school, before the eventful eve of eighth grade even, and ever after that memorable night had nibbled at the edge of her social circle like a nearly-sated pike, waiting for hunger to strike. I floated, submerging my intent in deep water, hoping, forever finning. Of course I had known since the womb and maybe before, that, in those days as now, an Ojibwe lad did not date a curly-headed blonde.

It was her parents' place away back. I launched a canoe from the reservation side of *Ginoogamaa*, "the lake is long." She had a different dog then, same breed as she always would. My sight was so sharp then, I didn't have to cross the lake to fish and watch. Hell, at that time I could tell an eagle from a hawk a couple miles away, saw mosquitos resting on leaf bottoms from twenty paces. So I watched. I fished. I started out earlier than she. The fishing was better before dawn, but I waited for cabin lights to come on to drift in her direction. Like members of the same family, thankfully, we were early risers, more so in the high days of summer. Restless, I guess.

In good weather, she brought breakfast to the dock. She carried a tray, the dog tripping at her heels, like me, hoping, and, once at the end of the dock, she set her meal down, keeping herself between the dog and the tray. She crouched, demurely I thought, touched the boards with her fingertips, and canted onto her palms, unfurling those legs over the water.

All the time the dog waited for its share of the food.

Riley slipped her shoes off one after the other, reaching now over the water, then lowered and dipped one tiny, slim foot then, with the other, cut the ripples she'd already made, slicing through the sparkling reflection of sun. Even back then, as farsighted as I was, I couldn't see the circlets she sliced, but what vision didn't reveal, imagination served. All the time, the spaniel waited.

At that distance I kept fishing, looking like I was trolling, dipping a paddle, pulling a J stroke, stirring the surface, gliding this way then that, trailing a line at the stern, my nose always pointing to her dock. Fishing was like breathing, and I could regard her while doing either. From the corner of one eye, I followed the water as I pulled. My stroke created a flatness on the lake's surface trailed by a small maelstrom that reached back to a string of others I'd laid over the lake all eventually melding with the rings Riley stirred up with her feet. One liquid spirit embracing the other.

Riley knew as well as I did that I was there, that I was eying her, that I waited. Neither of us, the lake being long, openly rippled or cut the private pool of the other: she never waved, she did not stare, and though not aloof, for years she did not acknowledge me other than to send out circles into the lake.

Once, perhaps trolling in too closely, I snagged my line on something at the bottom of the drop-off. Any fisherman worth his salt would have backstroked the way he'd drifted, but Riley had seated herself on the dock in that direction, and I did not dare approach. Neither did I want to admit to myself or show her that I'd caught a snag near her dock. I worked the line a while, praying the hook would come loose, let out more line than I wanted to lose just to improve the distance between us, and when far off enough for anything less than hawk eyes, I admitted that the root or stump or whatever it was held me in thrall had won a decisive victory. Looking the opposite way to appear innocent, I reached over and cut the line.

After that I would not allow myself to come so close. Though once, I broke this and another rule that I'd laid down after my sight began to fail—don't go out past sunset other than on moonlit nights. That time, during a monstrous storm, I dragged the drowning man I'd rescued up onto Riley's beach. For her and for me that was a momentous exception.

On the first visit of the wolves, a blind, overcast dawn called me from my old man's achy bed, and the fortunate rise of wind at my stiff back steered me like gravity across the bay in her direction. That morning breeze pushed me near as if I were the dawn itself. Even so, wrapped in the cataract of my night, I mistook the she wolf for Riley's dog, oddly out alone at early light. When the sandy-brown wolf's huge, dark mate came gliding around the cabin corner—I stupidly squinted against my nascent blindness—I at first thought he would attack the dog. He was a bristling silhouette, dark and tense. Then with no acknowledgment or exchange I could sense from either, acting in tandem, they raised snouts and tested the air. Then I knew them. Wolves. Spirits.

But like anything at all I'd ever realized and tried to hold to, after scenting once in their rapt pause at the cabin's porch-door screen, they turned to deep gray vapor, wisping into the stand of white pine beyond the house. I knew why they came, why they sniffed at the screen, but I didn't learn, though I feared then, for whom.

I'd met Riley early in my life, well before the carnival, but that was always the time I'd recall. Over forty years, the memory grew crisper as my sight dimmed.

Coming over the rise a two-mile walk from the Rez, the carnival spread before me, dazzling incandescent and neon lights, swirling. They looked to me like sun on windy water. The whirling colors seemed to twine with each other. I looked into the faces of my family sprayed by shafts of rainbow-like brilliance as if to ask, "Is this real?"

Mak, my oldest brother, laughed in his husky, quiet way and said, "Yes, little brother, this is heaven." *Makade-ma'iingan*, Black Wolf, joked always with everyone, but especially with me. Later they said he'd done his comedy show once too many times. The police didn't get it, but my sister told me that he kept the other Stillwater inmates in stitches for years. That came later. Now, Mak patted my shoulder to remind me that his words were light and were just for me.

I was ten, quite old for my first time at a carnival that visited town twice a year, Memorial and Labor Days. But we had our own celebrations and powwows. Maybe Mak and our mother thought it was time since in just days I'd move to junior high, into a bigger world. Maybe they had some cash left over from my father's Prudential debit policy and wanted to show Dad's orphan a good time. Whatever their reasons, I followed them, trusting deeply, working very hard to understand this new magic and to keep my sudden lust for its allure hidden from them, especially from Mak.

"Here," Mak said, extending three dollar bills—more than I'd ever before held in my hand. "Don't spend it too fast." He pointed into the darkness under high-reaching elms, beyond the flashes of orange and purple light. "We'll be down by the pond with George and them. Have fun." They left me in the middle of the midway, bewitched, dazzled, and rich. I rolled two bills up, slipping them into my shirt pocket. The other I folded into my jeans where I could feel it burning to get out. I stepped forward, gathering gumption like *manomin*, wild rice, pounding the stalks of my legs on the pavement, chuffing kernels of courage into the bottom of my queasy stomach.

I found I didn't need bravery. The magic carpet of mechanical wheels, arms, and rails floated me into the milling crowd, sprinkled by a sacrament of screaming laughter from above. I felt drunk on the torrid spirit.

Under a fluorescent-lighted canopy, I was hypnotized by boxes of articulating cranes, each clawing a pile of corn kernel and treasure behind its glass front that spilled golden light from the trove onto the face of its human operator. Each face at his box tensed, serious then went wild in anguish or joy. Mostly, as I watched, the faces mouthed disgust as a watch or ring slipped from the loose talons of the crane back onto the heap. With each failure, or success, the booth-man stuffed the booty deep back into the pile.

The fully-bearded man wearing a top hat leaned over a glass box at the corner of the booth. "Want to give it a try, kid?"

I stared at him, dumb.

"I'll give you a free trial," he said in a friendly way. "Just crank that handle there." He pulled a string behind the box and said, "Go."

I turned the wheel furiously, gripping its little stem. My crane rose lively enough, opening its claws, and swung so fast over the pile of treasure that it clunked the glass right in front of my face. I flinched. The shovel teeth clamped shut and fell atop a miniature car, useless to grab it.

"Reel it in, boy." The beard said.

I did this and the crane lifted again and rotated up and over to its original place.

"One try a dime, three for a quarter." The man extended a huge palm. When I hesitated he coaxed me, "Turn the handle gently, pause, then let 'er drop over something good." He cupped his palm, then, again.

I laid the hot dollar in his hand. "Three." The dollar was gone, and the top hat slapped three quarters on the box top. Those I whisked into my pocket. After my third failure the man returned. He tapped the top of the box with a coin. "You're getting the hang of it. Another go?"

I reached for my pocket, but Mak's words stopped me. I backed away. The bearded man turned to a tall, blond kid who tapped the glass with his quarter. In reverse, I ran smack into a woman's huge purse. "Hey, watch it there Jigaboo," said the man with her, swiping his hand at me. He missed, and I slipped into the crowd.

I wanted to disappear into the darkness that had swallowed my mother and Mak, down to the pond. I couldn't do that, yet. My cheeks burned hotter than the quarters I now clutched in my sweaty palm. I walked carefully now, picking my way down the midway, watching what others were doing.

Men, mostly young but looking full-grown to me, swaggered along in groups, jawboning loudly. A few strolled apart with an arm draped around a woman's shoulders. Others promenaded his arm linked with hers. Together they crowded the fair's main street. They jammed the booths on each side. In groups the men contested with each other, whipping balls fiercely at stuffed cat-dolls at one booth or trying to topple stacked concrete milk bottles at another. They guffawed at one another's misses and cheered the hits. The women stood back, out of arm's reach, oohing and ahhing the prowess of their men. Some girls took coins from purses to "toss 'n win" plates next tent over and, in the one just across the way, to roll change down wooden slots, jumping up and down to encourage the nickel to settle on a double or triple payoff space on the table.

"Got to roll to win, kid," the woman behind the checkerboard table said to me. Her cheeks were round, like Mother's.

"I'm just watching," I said. I studied the board, crosshatched by thick lines, and what folk were doing to win. A player cued up his coin in a slotted ramp, let gravity take the coin, usually a quarter, down the incline in hope it would roll, spin, and settle in a pay-off square somewhere on the table without touching one of the lines.

"Got to roll to win, kid," the woman repeated.

It looked easy. I gave her a quarter. "Five nickels, please."

"Big time roller here, folks," she crowed. Her cheeks jiggled above loose jowls.

My first nickel rolled over the payoff boundary line on the woman's side of the table. She picked it up. Pocketed it. I adjusted the direction of the little slotted ramp and rolled another.

"Big winner," she yelled. "Five times five!"

My next roll paid off fifteen cents, and the next double.

"Easy winner here. Take a lesson from the Ojibwe professor."

A crowd pressed in behind me. Now, my entire body roasted, hot from my toes to fingertips. I rolled twice and lost, then once more. The coin shot down the chute, curled on edge around the board, and spun, hovering in the dollar payoff square. It came to rest there.

"On the line!" The woman shouted and swept the nickel into her hand.

The crowed around booed her cheat. "Pay the kid off. It didn't even touch the line." People shouted and moved closer to reach the woman's arm.

She was outgunned and gave in. "Big brave wins a dollar! Twenty time winner!" Every one cheered.

"Do it again," a guy next to me said.

I counted the coins left in my hand, gathered the prize from the table, and I let those 20 nickels slide into my pocket.

"You're hot, boy, keep rolling," the vendor said.

Someone placed a gentle hand on my shoulder. "Luck never rushes, Paddler." It was Beaver, our cousin. "Let's walk."

We drifted away. I heard the hawker and the crowd groan.

"She wants her money back," Beaver chuckled.

He guided me up the midway toward the music of the carousel. "Have you tried the rides?" Beaver took me to a booth that resembled an outhouse. "Buy a couple of bucks worth of tickets and ride." He pointed to the merry-go-round, then the Tilt-a-Whirl and Ferris wheel. "That's good fun. Rides don't cheat you. Get in line and give the guy one ticket. See you later by the pond." He was gone.

I watched him fade into the crowd and lost sight of him as he descended the bank to the shadows surrounding the turtle pond.

I turned to a fleeting touch on my shoulder, light like a butterfly brushing past.

"Hi, Paddy." It was Riley standing at my back in the ticket line. She used my family nickname. How she knew it, I still don't know.

I've never been much for words outside of writing and jawing with my family, and basking so close to the person I'd loved from afar inspired every part of me except language. It fell to Riley to carry both of us in conversation. And she was ready.

"I'd love to go on some rides with you. Lynda is meeting me later, but she doesn't go for twirling anyway. Makes her dizzier." She laughed. Riley took my hand in hers and pulled me back into the line. "I'll get my tickets."

"I've got some," I said raising the fist that clutched the sheaf I'd bought.

"Dutch treat," she said. I didn't understand.

She moved to the barred window. "We each pay for the other. How many do you have?"

The ticket vendor told her, "Twenty."

I found my voice. "Should we ride the merry-go-round?"

She smiled back at me. I nearly died. "The Ferris wheel is my favorite, but the carousel is a good place to start."

With that night my trolling at the lake was born. Of course, I'd been out fishing plenty, but now I had a hidden purpose, waiting below the lake's drop-off for a sweet minnow. I'd have to look like I was fishing even when I was doing something entirely different. Fishing spreads its few rewards far apart. I trolled Riley's bay with like results.

After that night at the carnival, Riley seemed close at times, at others distant as Canada, and unattainable on any occasion. The strength of feeling, rising from a deep I had hardly before sensed, frightened me as much as had the carnival itself but drew me closer instead of repelling me. For the first few weeks after our chance adventure sharing tickets, and starting the very next day, the Tuesday following Labor Day, after sitting in the same classroom with Riley for three hours in the morning, I trolled the lake in the evenings. I caught more crappies than sights of Riley. In fact, the only time I spotted her on her dock during those late summer days, she had already turned toward her parent's cabin. If she saw me, she made no sign.

Later that fall, once ice began to form, first overnight, disappearing in each day's sun, finally skinning the entire lake thinly, not strongly enough to walk on, I was forced to give in to the change of season and content myself riding the school bus—I kept to the back, always—and sharing English and social studies class with her where I sat in front under the teacher's scrutiny. In class, I'd steal glances back at her to no effect.

On the dock mornings and evenings, though, she took on the special glow I'd sensed first in carnival light. Always, after that first evening, I regarded Riley from a distance. It was as if our Ferris wheel rides had happened in another life. Still, something about Riley's manner convinced me that she had shared that terrifying emotion that drew one close and repelled at once, like the whipping of the Tilt-a-Whirl we'd ridden.

We had begun that carnival night separated by the merry-go-round ticket-gate. I remained in line while

Riley, yelling "Yippee!" from her flying horse each time she arced by, rode without me. The next ride, I counted the empty saddles and kept next to her in line to make sure we both got on. That time, the platform filled rapidly, and in my confusion about what to do, I had to snag a stationary horse two courses behind her. Still she was fun to watch, turning in her saddle to call back at me. We learned to wait at the head of the line for the following ride to be able to choose mounts beside each other. We spent nearly half our tickets that way. Each time she gently pressed her ticket into my hand, and I did the same for her.

If anyone had called this puppy love, I would have grown angry. Even though I stayed true to that first immersion, like a holy baptism, Riley and I were never a couple. The experience did not stop me from finding a mate, having two children— although this came much later—or from experiencing a long and mature love and marriage. By the same token, that encounter—among many we shared but always at a distance—never faded or lessened from the day it had marked me.

Some say love strikes like lightning, but only once. Others tell us it is a solitary experience, unanchored to the loved one. Old tales sing of many affections that the wise one shall do nothing about but one. We can join in several loves only at a distance.

If I was a private fool all those years, I accept it and stand pat. Years later, the day the wolves were drawn to Riley's screen door, fright overcame me in another way. If they'd come calling for that something I'd never had, then the little I'd tried to keep might be taken away.

Yes, I married an *Anishinabe* woman. We lived at

the lake next to my mom. Poppy, my wife, would never acknowledge what she knew I saw just across the lake. My vision was less than real, of course, and phantoms and spirits are not meant to be shared, only experienced. Like the wolves, this spirit born at the carnival would turn to mist were I to grasp for it. That was it: my Riley, to me, lived in a spirit world, had always, and likely would disappear from it had I set foot on her dock. I came to believe it, because I trespassed that boundary once in a storm that for good or for bad sanctioned the breach, perhaps ordained the visit through its stronger spirit. Even so, after the storm that forced me to act a hero, the part of my life regarding Riley grew more complicated and more tightly entwined than ever.

The evening I landed on Riley's dock, I had paddled back from Hidden Bay on the south end of the lake. I hadn't hurried. I knew the wind at my back driving the black thunderheads my way would push me home when I cleared the narrows. Actually I was waiting for the blow to ease my effort past Riley's dock and homeward, too.

Waves crashing on the shore behind me deafened me to the rush of rising wind. The towering rain-makers and the gush of cold air came upon me much faster than I'd ever thought possible. Then everything changed. The surface of the lake ahead of me moved from placid to pock-marked and roiling in a second. Hail sliced the torrent of wind. I steadied the canoe as it shot out through the neck of water between shores into the bay. The gale cracked trees, felling their tops on the nearest bank behind me.

Immediately out of the narrows, a towering waterspout swirled me around and lifted the canoe out of the water. At the first tug of wind, when I saw that tornado, I'd locked my paddle under the seat and tossed my body down to twine myself between the stern and mid thwarts of the canoe. The funnel drew my craft up vertically, spinning it like a dervish, then, thrown out of the tornado from a height of perhaps thirty feet, the canoe sluiced stern first into the troubled lake, spilling all my gear—the tackle box hit my forehead—and filled with water from stern to bow as it was driven into the lake.

I had wedged myself to stay with the canoe, but now wished I'd worked free. The momentum the craft gained from the whirling spout and its three-story fall drove it beneath the surface of the lake toward the soft bottom. Had I time, I might have imagined the huge walleyes scattering in the deeps, looking for cover. If I'd been in a shallower place, the force would have lodged the canoe and me into the mucky bottom. But the deep water past the drop-off slowed, then, stopped us, and my boat and I, both holding our breath, finally rose to the surface.

I'd never prayed for Styrofoam before but praised it now and Grumman, too, for filling the draft with its buoyancy. The canoe and I floated toward the surface, gaining momentum over a few seconds, finally breaking the turbid waves. I bailed with my hands and then slapped water out with the only item saved, the paddle, all the while watching the spout skitter away over the water swirling and weaving like a drunkard. Detritus and loose trash, some of it mine, followed the funnel and some hung in the trees, flapping a warning too late to heed. Knifing in the thwarts below the surface had saved me after all from being thrown into the treetop across the narrows. Ahead of me, the waterspout grabbed another craft, a motor boat, flipping it over, the motor still running, screaming in the air. The force of the collision tossed a man out of the stern and into the water. The heavy boat landed upside down over him. I paddled with the wind to get there to help.

Through the rain pouring in sheets everywhere I saw the man surface, grab the gunwale of the boat. The outboard motor had stopped. I yelled into the torrent. He must have heard, for he turned toward me. He was hatless with blood washing down his face. His grip on the boat gave way, and he sunk from my sight. I made for the stern, lashed my canoe to the prop stanchion, and tossed my shoes forward in the canoe. The man rose again, sputtering and grasping for anything, but his face slipped under water.

I jumped for his boat, slid off its upturned belly to the water, and grabbed under his arms circling his torso with my legs. I pulled for all I was worth on the boat's keel and up he came, fighting me like I was the storm itself.

I had to shout. "I've got you! Relax!" That was all it took. We bobbed together between his overturned boat and my water-laden canoe. The gash on his forehead bled like the torrent that had just blown through. He'd be too weak to swim, even with help.

"We need the canoe. Hang on this side, I'll go under," I yelled. After I was sure he had a grip on the gunwale, I dipped under the bow and grasped the opposing edge.

"On three, pull yourself up just a bit." I counted, and now we looked at each other over the craft's sides. "Again on three, lock your elbows and flip a leg over the side." Fortunately, though dazed, he was able to do as I said. I'd reached across to steady his leg.

"Now, on three roll into the canoe." He was heavier than me, and though we didn't capsize, we rocked hard to his side, taking on more water. I tugged at my side, vaulted all the way in and hooked him by his belt to haul him into the bottom. Then I bailed like mad. Styrofoam or no, we needed less weight inside.

"Untie us up there," I shouted. He struggled with the knots first, then unsheathed a filet knife fastened to his belt to cut the rope.

"You bail. I'll paddle." I headed upwind for a dock where a figure bundled in a rain coat waved madly. It was Riley. I had her husband, Tib, bailing in the bow of my canoe.

So in that way, I came to her dock unbidden. She'd seen it all from her deck windows and had run out to take up a dock-hook. When I made a close enough pass, she captured the canoe and pulled us down the length of the dock to the shoals. There we were safe. I leapt from the stern to push us further up the shore. And when I slogged to the bow to tug it further, Riley was there to help.

Together we grounded the boat. Immediately and without hesitation, she circled my waist in her arms and hugged me hard.

"You are my paddler. Bless you," she said.

She turned to Tib. She wiped his brow and inspected. "Bloody but not too deep," she said. We heaved him up, now spent and barely conscious, between the two of us, her husband listing toward Riley's smaller stature, and lugged him out of the craft and up to the cabin. Somehow she bore his weight.

I did not feel like a hero. As soon as I realized who I'd saved, my guilt dripped over the welcome mat of Riley's cabin where I held Tib up as she opened the door. I could have let him slide down to death, I thought. That idea, chaste but evil, I would carry beside my image of Riley on our Ferris wheel ride until wolves came for one of us.

I could never again separate our carnival ride from that selfish, storm-driven death wish.

In fact, when those very wolves did come, I thought it was me who had summoned them through my evil thoughts as old as those wishes had become. The spirit world considers a long time before it acts, either that or they are very busy over there. But I was wrong. That first time nosing around the door, they came for Riley's dog. For a long while after, she stood on the dock—she did not sit now as she had in youth—looking, I thought, the length of the lake or further. Soon winter obscured everything again. When the thaw was complete and the docks were out again, she had another spaniel.

At the carnival, Riley and I abandoned the carousel for the excitement of the Tilt-a-Whirl. On half a dozen rides, we smashed together, squeezed into one or the other corners of the arced seat, then slid the other way across, banging the opposite cushion. Twirling one way, her slender frame jammed into my meaty bones, reversing direction I pressed her between the side cushion and my fatty bulk. I enjoyed both contacts, but pulled against the force to avoid suffocating her. She felt good against me. We exited and stood dizzy in the midway.

"You have four tickets left?" She said. "I want you to take me on the Ferris wheel."

I tipped my head back to take in the height of the giant wheel. My knees and stomach grew weak.

"Come on." Riley took my hand behind her, placing it at her hip, and draped her other arm around my back to reach my far shoulder. As if still spinning in a padded carriage, we sauntered and pressed to one another toward the towering wheel.

I had climbed trees with friends only when goaded, but I'd never been on a rooftop or up the stairs of the fire tower in the forestry station, never really been off the ground. My feelings for Riley, though, pushed me to do that which I would have backed away from in any other company. Still, once aboard I clutched the puny safety bar with fists tense as iron vises and braced myself rigidly between seat and foot-guard. Riley rested her hand now on my near shoulder and nestled to my side.

"Relax, Paddy. This will be fun."

When we rose in reverse from the boarding platform taking to the air, she stroked my hand and pried my fingers off the bar one by one. We stopped and our seat swung on its pivots.

"Whee, rock the cradle," she said, laughing.

I was miserable through most of the ride, until off-boarding began and we stopped at the top of the wheel. Riley took both my hands from the bar—she was careful not to rock our seat—and drew us together in a gentle hug.

"I've wanted to do this all night," she said.

I managed to say two words: "Me, too."

We rode again. I hoped we'd continue all the evening, maybe watch the fireworks from the top of this new world I'd entered. But as I was fingering the last two tickets left in my pocket, Riley's friend, Lynda, saw us in the line.

"There you are, Parsons."

"Hi, Lynda. Wait for me by the haunted house. We've got one more ride."

Once in our seat, I handed Riley my last ticket. "Take a ride with Lynda. I won't be needing this."

"No, you use it. Thank you for a wonderful time." I still have the lone ticket from that night. I've kept it in my wallet for almost fifty years now.

At the top of our last ride, we hugged and Riley looped her arms around my neck. "Thank you, Paddler." We kissed.

Next minute it seemed, I stood dumbly at the base of the great wheel, watching Riley diminish and pass into the crowd on her way to meet her friend.

After a few minutes, I followed in her direction past the haunted house, cutting down the hill into the darkness surrounding the pond, carrying a hope, a solitary ticket, and tingling lips, on my way to rejoin my family to watch the fireworks.

After Poppy died and my sight began to fail, I still carried an odd hope that the two hugs and the single kiss Riley and I shared would grow into something before the end of my fishing days. I never considered it ridiculous, though it may have been. Life and the time we spend in it is so corrosive of hope, so certain in its wearing down of one's spirit, that, especially in old age, a man grows liable to carry fantastic dreams in his creel. He transports impossibilities in mind far beyond his abilities, perhaps even beyond his grave. I didn't wish for Tib's death even an hour beyond the afternoon I had saved him. Despite the shame I felt every day since though, I was ready, I thought. I was poised, arthritic and nearly sightless as I was, for his spirit to forsake Long Lake forever.

When the wolves came that second time, then, I shamed myself and prayed. I did not ask for death, I hoped against it, but for Riley. Even though it was nearing true dusk as I was planted in my shoreline chair sensing everyone's light setting where mine already had, I knew without seeing that the frightful pair snooted and sniffed the door across the bay just up the walk from Riley's dock. A man who had stayed on a scent as long as I had has no need to regard the physical animals to know they are nearby.

The promise of the hours of the following dawn led me through a blind and torturous night. I'd prayed once in the storm. I would not do it again. What was left was waiting mixed with old hope.

I rose from an exhausted bed before the morning. I felt my way to the chair where I'd hung my clothes and then out the kitchen door where I'd strung a line down to my dock.

I felt mists on my face, hung still over the lake. Tired, sightless, worried, I sat in the canoe but could not launch. Even sixty years of dead reckoning would not find her dock. And gravity seemed to flow in the wrong direction. I waited for the first breath of dawning that moved the mist along, bristling tufts of it that always drifted along in the wannest of morning light. I dipped my paddle. Like the mists themselves, like the very dawn behind the stern, I moved in the old way into fear and hope.

I was close. I'd counted my stiff-armed strokes all the way across. I left off and glided in past the drop-off I knew so well. I heard the spaniel sound her alarm and sensed through a lifting mist the figure crouching to steady the dog with a jingling stroke across her collar. Then he touched the bow. It was Tib who rose and tied me to the post.

As the canoe swung from the end of the dock, I pushed the paddle bow-ward and came to rest. He knelt, I heard, beside the dog.

"She left this for you." He placed a cellophane envelope containing, I found later, two torn ticket stubs, reaching carefully to press it into my hand. "Can I bring you back home?" His voice was kind.

"Thank you," I said. "I will find my way." I slipped her gift into my jacket and pushed off. "I'm sorry."

Tib helped me turn the canoe straight toward the sunrise, the surest thing of the entire day.

What they say about your hearing growing sharp after the loss of sight seems right to me. Returning homeward the morning Riley died I saw, and even that was dim. After that all was shadow, then nothing. I began to hear things better, parsed from the dark background of what used to be sight. My nose tuned up quite a bit as well.

The first few days after paddling into sunrise, I stayed in bed, feeling my way to the toilet and refrigerator. I kept Riley's envelope tucked under the unused lamp stand on my reading table, afraid it would fall to the floor somewhere to disappear along with my sight.

After two nights and three days, my granddaughter came by. I'd heard her calls and messages, but would never have found the phone in time. My body had become incredibly heavy, lethargic.

When she finally came over, she said, "Are you sick, Paddy?"

"I'm blind, Sis."

Her weight depressed that side of the mattress. I felt her hand move the air just above my open eyes. "How many fingers?" She asked.

"Six."

"Hey, I'm serious. How many?"

"I cannot see even one. I'm blind."

"How long have you been in bed?"

"Since it happened. Yesterday, Tuesday."

"Today is Thursday It's six p. m. Have you eaten?"

"Yesterday."

She went to the kitchen. She was a good cook. Afterward she led me to the shower, tuned it to the right temperature.

"I'll leave a clean change of clothes on the chair right here." She took my hand to the chair back. "Toss the old ones on the floor. The soap and cloth are in there. The towel on top of the clothes." Again, she drew my hand there.

And so it went, Poppy's oldest child with me taught me how to see again, enough to get by with help, enough to find a chair in the afternoon sun, to find the radio, to find and keep the ticket stubs the love of my young life had kept for me.

In the mornings when the birds sing or the winter sun warms my bedroom some, I take them out, still housed in the cellophane, and touch them to my lips. I do that at sunset—whenever I think it is—and set them in the drawer again for tomorrow.

I've done that all through the winter. Listening for the birds, for the sigh of the wind at dusk, for my granddaughter's Chevy, for the lapping of the lake that separated Riley from me and joined us just the same.

This evening, even with Sis clattering in the kitchen, I heard a sound, familiar but somehow very far away.

"Sis, is someone at the door?"

She yelled back she didn't think so.

"Could you check? I think someone is outside."

Her voice curled around my doorway. "So you don't want to eat?"

"Yes. But please . . . ."

I heard her wiping her hands on the dishcloth. She

tossed it down. "All right already."

Sis stepped back down the hall after what seemed to a blind man a very long time. I felt her in the doorway of my bedroom. She came to the bed, sat and swung her arm across me to lean close in.

"Well," I said, "who was it?"

She didn't answer right away. I thought she was crying.

"Are you going to tell me?"

She placed her hands on mine and then she spoke.

"Wolves."

Wolf's End

As he circled—
his blind eye
turned away—
he scented a thing
reminiscent
of a moose carcass
in summer.
Of that whiff,
a solid effluvium
of terror in battle,
he paid no mind
for a steady eye
a quiet heart
a fierce muzzle
a lightning lunge
had always been
his armor
his love
his salvation.
Hardly could he have
known the odor
flowed out
over his bared fangs
held open
in their last lunge.

The ancient levies
weighed down.

Lake Stories and Other Tales is Tim Jollymore's fourth book.

A midlife transplant to The Northern California Bay Area, Jollymore still draws strength and stories from his native Minnesota and augments them with tales from across the West.

Jollymore holds a master of arts degree from the University of Minnesota and is a veteran teacher of writing in Oakland.

Acknowledgments

This work was possible only with the help of my advance readers and authors Davyd Morris, John Cox, Bruce Coyle, Kitty Fassett, and William Weinreb.

Eternal thanks and my love to Carol Squicci, designer and chief supporter in this effort.